HELL HATH NO FURY

Private investigator Sam Spain receives a visit from a little old lady who wants him to find her twenty-two-year-old daughter, Irene, who has been missing for a month. Sam learns that Hugo Dare, a racketeer-turned-politician, has supplied Irene with a bungalow on Eucalyptus Drive. From the moment Sam discovers a corpse in Irene's room, he runs into nothing but grief. Irene is in a jam, framed for murder. Sam hides the girl and goes on with his investigation. Then he finds himself in the same jam as Irene — framed for a murder he hasn't committed!

REX MARLOWE

HELL HATH NO FURY

Complete and Unabridged

LINFORD
Leicester

First published in Great Britain

First Linford Edition
published 2005

British Library CIP Data

Marlowe, Rex
    Hell hath no fury.—Large print ed.—
Linford mystery library
1. Detective and mystery stories
2. Large type books
I. Title
823.9′14 [F]

ISBN 1–84395–894–5

Published by
F. A. Thorpe (Publishing)
Anstey, Leicestershire

Set by Words & Graphics Ltd.
Anstey, Leicestershire
Printed and bound in Great Britain by
T. J. International Ltd., Padstow, Cornwall

This book is printed on acid-free paper

1

Sam Spain had his feet on the desk and his chair tilted back. Beside his feet there was a half-empty bottle of rye whisky. He held a dirty tumbler in his hand and sipped from it, alternately placing a lighted cigarette to his lips. Through the closed window behind him, sounds of mid-morning traffic echoed from San Francisco's Market Street.

The door was shut and the air held a fug of tobacco smoke. Lettering on the pebbled glass inset of the door told enquirers:

SAM SPAIN — Investigations Private

Only there weren't any enquirers, and it was altogether too private. Sam brooded. No investigations — no money. No money — no whisky, cigarettes, food, or anything else. His one-room apartment

1

didn't cost a lot, but this office did. He wondered where he was going to get next month's rent from. He even wondered why he bothered with the private investigation racket ... but he'd been over that too many times to worry any more.

San Francisco, like many other American cities, had too many cheap crooks bearing down on honest citizens; too many gunmen willing to murder for thirty pieces of silver; too many smart-alecs sitting back and getting rich on blackmail and robbery and murder. Sam didn't like the hatchetmen with tommy-guns and pine-apples who took protection money from hard-working shopkeepers; that's why he'd joined the force. To fight crime.

He'd been in the service five years and he had a good record, but an honest cop isn't always allowed to go after the men at the top of the rackets. There was too much political graft, too many civic leaders taking hush-money. Sure, there were plenty of honest, gang-busting cops, but they had their hands tied by crooked politicians. It hadn't taken Sam long to figure that.

He'd been too keen, too good at busting the rackets that kept councillor's pockets lined, so he'd been taken off the real jobs. He'd turned in his badge and gone freelance, applied for a private detective's licence. He'd got it — and a warning to keep his nose clean.

That was eighteen months back and now he had a reputation. A reputation for being an honest cop who fought for the rights of honest citizens, a man who couldn't be bought, a man as tough as the hoodlums he went after.

Sam didn't think of himself as a hero; he was just a tough guy who didn't like to see women beaten up and orphans starve because the breadwinner wouldn't pay protection money. It took a tough guy to stand up to killers; an honest man with a sense of duty and unshakable integrity. Sam Spain was such a man, and there weren't enough of them in San Francisco.

He brooded, leaning back in the chair and wondering why his services weren't in demand. He was five foot eight in his socks, tough as leather, and fit as an athlete. He had straight, dark hair and grey eyes. He was neither handsome nor rugged; his face was ordinary except for the taut lines about his mouth; and these made him look as if his face had been dipped in acid. He never smiled with his lips; they formed a thin, harsh line; only his eyes smiled, revealing a softer side to his character.

Footsteps sounded from the other side of the door; someone was crossing the reception room floor. There came a knock on the door. Sam's feet came off the desk, the whisky bottle and glass disappeared into a cupboard; he stubbed out his cigarette and opened the window half an inch to let out some of the fug.

'Come in,' he called.

The door opened to admit a little old lady. She was around sixty, with greying hair and a worried look to her lined face. She was dressed quietly in black relieved by a faded green hat which had been out of fashion for ten years. She didn't look as if she had a lot of money to throw around.

'Take a seat,' Sam said, opening the window wider.

She perched on the edge of the chair across the desk from Sam.

'Mr. Spain?' she asked. Her voice trembled a little.

Sam nodded.

'I'm Mrs. Kline, Mr. Spain. A friend of mine told me you were an honest man, that you'd help me.'

Sam's grey eyes smiled. It was a long time since anyone had called him Mr. Spain.

'It's nice to have friends,' he said softly. 'How can I help you?'

She hesitated, pulled some money from her handbag.

'It's all I have, Mr. Spain. I hope it will be enough.'

Sam looked at her carefully. He varied his rate according to his client.

'My time costs ten dollars a day plus expenses. I'll take fifty dollars retainer. That comes out of the final bill.'

He'd like to have cut it more, but he still had to pay the rent at the end of the month. She handed him five ten-dollar bills and pushed the rest back in her handbag.

'I want you to find my daughter, Irene. She's disappeared.'

'Job for the police,' Sam said.

Mrs. Kline smiled faintly.

'I reported it, of course, but the man I saw didn't seem very hopeful. He said they had thirty disappearances a week. I've been to her apartment; she moved without leaving a forwarding address. I went to the club where she worked but the manager wouldn't see me. The man at the door couldn't help.'

'Suppose,' suggested Sam gently, 'that you start at the beginning?'

He lit a fresh cigarette and waited. Mrs. Kline folded her hands in her lap but that didn't stop Sam noticing she was nervous. Her voice told him that.

'I come from Paradise Valley, in Nevada, Mr. Spain. It's a quiet place and nothing much happens. I guess it was too quiet for Irene because when dad died, two years ago, she left home and came to San Francisco. She had a number of jobs, waitress, dishwasher, clerk, anything she could get, and she used to send me money each week.'

'A nice girl,' Sam commented. His tone was flat. He knew what happened to nice girls who lived alone in the big city.

Mrs. Kline nodded.

'Irene's a good girl, she wouldn't do anything — wrong. She was brought up to behave decently, but she has a wild streak in her. She got that from dad. Her last job was hat-check girl at the 400 Club.'

Sam's eyes weren't smiling. He knew the 400 Club and the men who used it. He wouldn't want any girl of his working there, not even checking in hats. Mrs. Kline went on:

'She sent me a bit more money while she was there. Then, a month ago, she stopped sending me anything. My letters went unanswered. Two days ago, I decided to come to San Francisco myself, to find out what had happened to her. Even if she'd lost her job and couldn't send money, she'd have written me. I'm sure of that, Mr. Spain.'

Sam was sure too. He could tell what

7

sort of girl Irene was, just from looking at her mother.

'She'd left her apartment,' Mrs. Kline said, 'and the man at the 400 Club wouldn't tell me anything. I'm worried about her, Mr. Spain. She's all I've got in the world and I don't want anything to happen to her. I want you to find her for me, to bring her home.'

Sam smoked his cigarette without tasting it. He wanted to know something about Irene and he didn't want to insult Mrs. Kline. He couldn't remember his own mother, but if she'd been anything like Mrs. Kline, she'd have been tops with Sam.

'Have you a photograph?' he asked.

Mrs. Kline fumbled with her bag. She produced a cheap pic, the sort that street-photographers take while you're strolling along the promenade with your best girl friend. Only Irene was alone.

'It was taken a year ago, here in San Francisco.'

Sam could tell that from the backdrop, a view of the Dutch windmill in Golden Gate Park. He saw a young, slim girl with a nice figure and a pretty face. Irene wasn't a glamour girl, but she was pretty enough to turn men's heads. She was wearing a cotton print dress and wedge-shoes, and she had no ring on any of her fingers.

'Describe her to me,' he commanded. 'Colour hair, distinguishing marks, that sort of thing.'

Mrs. Kline closed her eyes and leaned back a little, concentrating. She said, slowly:

'Irene has red hair and reddish-brown eyes. A nice-looking girl. She never used much make-up. She's twenty-two.'

She paused.

'I don't know how to describe her, Mr. Spain. I suppose a mother never really looks at her daughter.'

Sam nodded.

'I know how it is. You take the people around you too much for granted.' His voice changed, became flatter. 'Any birth-marks or anything of that kind?'

Mrs. Kline looked as if she didn't want to answer that. Sam leaned forward and the lines about his mouth tightened.

9

'I'm broadminded, Mrs. Kline — and girls who disappear have a nasty habit of turning up on a slab in the morgue. If she's alive I won't need to see anything I shouldn't.'

Mrs. Kline shuddered.

'Irene has a crescent-shaped scar on her left leg.' She blushed. 'On her thigh.'

'I hope I won't need that identification,' Sam said. 'Where was she living when you last heard?'

'1657a Felton Street. She had a room in an apartment house.'

Sam stubbed out his cigarette. He got up, closed the window. He glanced out and down. Market Street was jammed with people and the city stretched north and south, east and west. A big city with a big population. He turned away from the window, his grey eyes smiling.

'I'll find her, Mrs. Kline, so you can stop worrying. Where can I get in touch with you again?'

The little old lady moved to the door.

'I'm staying at the Alameda, near the station.'

She had her hand on the door knob

10

when Sam said, casually:

'Any men friends?'

Mrs. Kline shook her head.

'There was no-one,' she replied. 'Irene would have told me if there had been.'

Sam nodded. He hoped Irene was as nice as her mother thought she was, but nice girls can change, alone in a big city. He hoped nothing had happened to her; there were houses down by the waterfront and not all the girls were there from choice.

'You'll be hearing from me,' he said as Mrs. Kline went through the reception room to the passage.

Sam took another slug of whisky. He was working again. A small job, but you could never tell where it might lead. Remembering a similar job that had taken him into the heart of a snatch racket, he strapped on a shoulder-holster and snapped a magazine into his Luger. It was because he went into action prepared for trouble that Sam Spain was still in the detective business.

2

The Ford was old and battered but life still hummed under the bonnet. The paintwork was flaking off in places and the upholstery needed patching, but Sam wouldn't have changed the car for a new one. He was used to the old Ford, had the feel of the car — besides it had cost him a hundred bucks to have bullet-proof glass fitted.

He cruised down Van Ness, cut through to Potrero Avenue, then on to Bay Shore Boulevard. He crossed Silver Avenue and turned right, into Felton Street. The houses were gaunt and packed too close together; strings of washing hung between the drab brick and concrete blocks; there was a smell.

1657a was no different from the others. Sam parked his car and went up the steps. The door opened at a push and he found himself in a gloomy hallway. Over a window in the left-hand wall, a notice proclaimed:

Ring for Service

Sam pushed the bellpress and waited. Nothing happened so he knocked on the glass window. It opened after a while and a face with white hair and yellow teeth showed. It was a woman's face but you had to look hard to be sure.

'Single room three dollars a week. Pay in advance and no funny business. That means no girl friends — this is a respectable house.'

Sam laid his private detective's licence on the ledge.

'I don't want a room,' he said. 'I'm looking for a girl who used to board here. Irene Kline, a red-head, twenty-two, pretty but not beautiful, slim. Remember her?'

The woman looked at Sam and sniffed. 'What's she done?'

Sam pushed a folded dollar bill across the ledge. It vanished instantly.

'I want to know where I can find her, that's all. As far as I know, she hasn't done anything. This isn't a police job.'

The woman considered a moment.

'I remember,' she said. 'Her mother was around yesterday, looking for her.'

Sam nodded.

'That's right. Irene seems to have disappeared. Mrs. Kline hired me to find her.'

The woman said:

'Wish I could help you. She just packed her things and walked out one day. Didn't leave any forwarding address.'

Sam pushed another folded bill across the ledge. The woman said, sharply: 'That's the truth. I'd tell you if I knew — I liked the girl.'

Sam thought a moment, then said:

'Tell me about Irene. What sort of girl was she? Have any men friends? Pay you all right?'

'She was okay, was Irene,' the woman said. 'Paid regular and never gave any trouble. A nice girl, she didn't fool around with the wrong kind of men — any kind of men, for that matter. I hope nothing's happened to her.'

Quite a girl, Sam thought. She's too good to be true.

'I'll leave my card,' he said. 'If she turns up, get in touch with me.'

'Sure, I'll do that.' The woman pushed Sam's two dollar bills back across the ledge. 'I don't want your money — keep it for someone who won't talk without. I liked Irene. I'd help you if I could, mister.'

Sam went down the steps to his car. He got behind the wheel and nosed the Ford into the traffic on Bay Shore Boulevard. He went up Potrero Avenue, along 10th Street to Van Ness. He passed the City Hall and kept on north, across California and Pacific to Marina Boulevard. He swung left and found the 400 Club opposite Marina Park.

Sam knew the manager, Ambrose Muir, and hoped he wouldn't make trouble. Muir was like that. He ran a high-class nighterie, with girls and gambling tables; how he kept inside the law was his affair. The cops had never caught him out, but only because he was too clever to make a slip.

Sam flashed his card at the doorman and went through swing glass doors. The club was quiet at this hour of the day. Cleaners were busy removing the empty bottles and cigar butts; two cabaret girls were doing a routine with the pianist; the chromium and tiled room had shed its glamour. There was a man propped against the bar.

A slim man wearing a drape suit with padded shoulders. His hands were long and slender and his complexion olive. His skin was slightly greasy, his eyes dark and watchful. He moved forward as he saw Sam, hunching his padded shoulders.

'What d'you want, Spain?' he said coldly.

Sam's grey eyes smiled humorlessly. He knew that Cabot carried a gun for Muir.

'A word with the boss. Give me no trouble and I'll give you none.'

Cabot said: 'Yeah?'

He didn't like cops, private or otherwise. He looked at Sam, considering him thoughtfully. Then he shrugged.

'I guess it's okay for you to see the boss. But mind what you say — he's kind o' particular. In front of me, through the arch.'

Sam let his hands dangle loosely as he preceded Cabot through the archway back of the club, along a passage to a door marked:

MANAGER

Cabot knocked and a voice said:
'Who is it?'
'Cabot. Sam Spain wants to see you.'
There was a pause, then the door opened and Sam stared at the slight figure of Ambrose Muir. He had fair hair and cold blue eyes and his professional smile was absent as he greeted Sam.
'Well, Spain, what is it?'
Sam pushed into the office. His eyes flickered round the room, noting the thick pile on the floor, the inlaid desk and swivel chair. There was a cocktail bar in one corner, a steel safe in another.
He took out a cigarette, lit it, making Muir wait for his reply. He wanted the night club manager on edge. He blew a stream of smoke into Muir's face and the manager stepped back, coughing.
Cabot jabbed Sam in the ribs.
'Cut that out,' he grunted. 'We don't

like tough guys here. Say your piece and get out.'

Sam said: 'I'm looking for a girl who used to work here. Irene Kline. She checked in hats. Maybe you'd know where she hangs out?'

Muir stared at him in disgust.

'You think I keep tabs on all the girls who work here?' he asked. 'She left about a month back. Just walked out without a word. I've no idea where she is — and care less!'

'No need to take that attitude,' Sam pointed out 'This is a friendly call. I'm not after you, Muir — unless anything has happened to her. She's disappeared.'

'That so?' Muir said. He shrugged. 'It happens.'

'Yeah,' Cabot repeated flatly, 'it happens!'

Sam puffed at his cigarette. Something told him these men knew more than they were giving out.

He said: 'It doesn't happen to girls like Irene. She was a nice girl.'

They didn't say anything. Sam asked:

'She friendly with any man around the club?'

Muir was amused.

'How would I know? Some of the girls like mink coats and diamonds, some don't. I wouldn't know about Irene — she was only a hat check girl.'

'Yeah,' said Cabot, grinning, 'a hat check girl. I remember her, now. A redhead — ' his hands moved in curves — 'so — so, nothing to get excited about.'

It was an elaborate façade. They knew, but they weren't telling.

'Maybe someone got excited about her,' Sam said casually.

'Maybe,' Muir replied.

There was another silence. Sam felt as if he had run into a brick wall. Then Muir said:

'Sorry, I can't help you, Spain.'

It was a smooth dismissal. Sam turned to the door and paused.

'I'll be back,' he said grimly, 'if anything's happened to her.'

Cabot followed him out into the passage, then Muir's voice came:

'Cabot! I want to talk to you — Spain can find his own way out.'

The slim man shrugged and turned

back. He entered Muir's office and closed the door behind him leaving Sam alone in the passage. Sam went on down the passage, on his way out, when a low whistle stopped him.

He turned to see a blonde head peeping round the door. A bare arm waved to him. Sam went back to see what she wanted.

'Inside, quick,' the girl said.

Sam moved into a dressing room and the girl closed the door softly behind him. There was a smell of powder and scent in the air and scanty costumes hung on hooks. Sam looked at the blonde.

She had a nice shape and not much covering it, but that didn't seem to worry her. She sat down in a chair before a table-mirror and stared thoughtfully at Sam.

'The door was open,' she said in explanation. 'I heard you asking for Irene.'

Sam showed interest, but the blonde wasn't in a hurry.

'What's it worth?' she asked.

Sam folded a dollar bill and passed it to

her. She tucked the note away in the top
of a nylon stocking and said:

'Chicken feed!'

Sam folded another bill and passed it
across.

'I'm not a gold-mine,' he remarked.
'Give!'

The blonde smiled vacantly.

'What have you got on her? I'm not
sure I want to talk to a shamus. Irene
never did anyone any harm.'

'That's the way I figure it,' Sam agreed.
'But maybe someone did her harm. She's
disappeared.'

'I heard you,' the blonde said.

Sam folded another dollar bill and
rustled it idly.

'Where is she? That's all I want to know.'

The blonde watched the note as if it
fascinated her.

'Might be anywhere,' she said.

Sam sighed and strolled towards the
door.

'You're wasting my time!'

She didn't like to see good money walk
out on her. She turned quickly, snapped:

'Don't be in such a hurry. I'll talk

— but this mustn't get back to Muir. Understand?'

Sam nodded. The blonde had her head screwed on; she didn't want to be fished out of the bay with her face slashed.

'Talking to me is like talking to a wall.'

'Even walls have ears!' she snapped.

'This one has,' Sam said, giving her the dollar bill.

The blonde went over to the door, edged it open. The passage was silent. She closed the door again, said:

'Try 212 Eucalyptus Drive.'

Sam lit a fresh cigarette and concentrated on blowing a smoke ring.

'That's a classy area for a hat check girl,' he commented.

The blonde smirked.

'I didn't say she was paying rent!'

Sam frowned.

'I don't see Irene playing that game,' he said slowly. 'You giving it to me straight?'

The blonde jeered at him.

'There comes a time in every girl's life . . . that prim miss stood off more wolves than a mushy love story heroine. The goddam fool! She wouldn't even let the customers pinch her legs, then she falls for Hugo Dare!'

Sam stiffened. He'd never met Hugo Dare, but he knew the name. Dare was a racketeer on his way up. He was supposed to have left his old ways behind, was going straight, running for election this year. A mobster moving in on politics, cleaning up big. If Irene was playing with Hugo Dare she was playing with dynamite and the explosion would take off more than her eyebrows.

'Tell me about that,' he said.

The blonde held out her hand. Sam slipped another greenback into it. He'd met some gold-diggers before, but this one worked overtime on it.

'Irene was the sort of girl you read about in Sunday supplements, old-fashioned, strait-laced. To her, men were either good or bad, and she didn't play around. She was right out of her element here — she should have stayed in Paradise Valley. Plenty of men tried to make her, but she gave them the freeze. Not that she was any glamour girl, but her figure was good enough to make men look twice. But they didn't get anywhere with Irene.'

The blonde crossed her legs and looked at Sam. He fed her another note and she ran on:

'She believed in love and Prince Charming. She was waiting for the right guy to come along. Then she'd marry him and raise a family. Only Hugo Dare came along . . . '

Sam knocked the ash from his cigarette and tried to figure out what Dare would see in a girl like Irene.

'It knocked me cold,' the blonde confessed. 'Of course, she didn't know anything about him, but even so — ' she drew a deep breath. 'She should have had more sense. She thought Dare was in love with her, wanted to marry her.'

She laughed harshly.

'A man like Dare doesn't fall in love. He just takes what he wants and Irene wasn't his type. That was the baffling part. Dare could have any glamour girl he wanted — and he did, one after another — so why should he waste time on a hat check girl?'

Sam admitted he didn't know. His lips formed a thin line, very taut; he had an idea Irene had walked into a load of grief.

'She fell for Dare like a ton of bricks, red-hot bricks at that,' the blonde said. 'She was crazy about the guy. It was love, the real thing. She was a sucker and Dare played her along. It was all very discreet; I guess not many people knew about her and Dare, which is another mystery. Why should he want to keep it secret?'

Sam didn't know that one either. He was getting worried about Irene. She had been missing a month, and a lot can happen in that time — and whatever game Hugo Dare was playing, he was playing for keeps. Maybe he would see that crescent-shaped scar after all.

'You're getting this cheap,' the blonde grumbled, and Sam folded another dollar bill and watched it disappear into the top of a nylon stocking.

'She went off with Dare, one day, and hasn't been back since. I happened to see the card Dare gave her. There was an address on it: 212 Eucalyptus Drive. I guess that's the lot.'

Sam stood up.

'I'll run over and see what's happening,' he said grimly.

'You'd better watch yourself,' the blonde cautioned. 'And leave me out of it!'

Sam nodded.

'Maybe I'll want to see you again. Who do I ask for?'

The blonde grinned.

'Just ask for Trixy. I'm always available . . . anything else I can do for you?'

Sam said: 'Not just now. Wrong end of the day for me.'

She flashed him a professional smile.

'Drop around and see me one night. I've kinda taken a fancy to you.'

Sam didn't reply. He was worrying about Irene Kline. He went along the passage and out into the street. Across the park, the waters of San Francisco Bay sparkled in the sunlight. He got into his Ford and drove south down Scott Street, past Alamo Square to the junction of Market Street and 17th. He swung right along Market Street to Portola Drive. Twin Peaks reared on his right, lofty grass-capped hills dominating the sky-scrapers and rows of apartment houses.

South of Sloat Boulevard, the houses straggled out, large houses in spacious grounds. A residential area if you were in the higher income brackets. Sam turned into Eucalyptus Drive and started hunting for 212.

He found it, a green-tiled bungalow, backed by sand-dunes. A short drive led between grass verges to the front porch. Trees, poplar and spruce, screened the bungalow from the other houses on Eucalyptus Drive. It was select, discreet. Irene must have noticed a violent change from her room in Felton Street.

Sam parked his car and walked up to the door. The bungalow was quiet, seemingly empty. He rang the bell and waited. No one answered so he went round the side, treading lightly on the gravel path, till he found a window. He forced it open and climbed through. He stood on a Persian carpet in a tastefully decorated living room, listening. No sound came. He moved forward, using his eyes all the time.

Someone had been here, and recently. A girl. Her scarf, silken and scented, lay draped across a leather padded chair. Sam opened a door and went out into the passage. A girl's coat and hat hung on the hall stand. He found the kitchen and looked in. The larder was well-stocked but no meal had been prepared that day.

A pair of silk stockings hung over a radiator in the bathroom. They had dried long ago. Sam went through the bungalow. Each room was expensively furnished; comfort was the key-note. Nothing had been spared to make the place a luxury home.

If Irene hadn't smelt a rat when she saw the set-up, she needed a new set of grey cells. Sam had stopped worrying about moving quietly; it was obvious the bungalow was empty or someone would have shown up by now. He tried the door of the last room, the bedroom.

A smell of scent and powder greeted him. A filmy negligee lay across a chair; feminine silk pyjamas in pastel blue were neatly folded on the dressing table, beside ivory and gold hair-brushes and a leather make-up case, mono-grammed I.K. Sam turned to the bed, a wide, double bed *with a dead man* sprawled across it.

3

The dead man was short and thick-set. His face was the colour of wax and he was stiff and cold; he had been dead about twelve hours, Sam guessed. The haft of an ice-pick protruded from the man's heart and his purple satin pyjamas were matted with dried blood. He had died instantly and his eyes were still open, fixed and horrible; his face told Sam, he had seen death coming.

Whoever he had been, it wasn't Hugo Dare. Sam had seen pictures of Dare and they were nothing like the corpse. The man's clothes were piled on a chair by the bed. Sam went through the pockets and found identification.

The name was Bartlett, Clint Bartlett of 11a Commercial Street. Sam found something else, a package of white powder. He sniffed it — heroin. There didn't seem to be anything else of importance, so Sam tidied up, wiping his prints off everything he'd touched. He'd got around to the window frame when he heard high heels on the porch and the sound of a key turning in the lock.

He went back to the passage as Irene Kline came through the front door. She gave a little gasp as she saw Sam.

'I'm a private investigator,' Sam said quickly. 'Your mother hired me to find you.'

He showed his licence to establish his identity, looking her over carefully. The photograph had been a good likeness. She was as tall as Sam, slim, with a good figure. Her face wasn't beautiful, pretty, with a minimum of make-up. Her hair was long and red like autumn leaves in the sunlight.

'Your mother was worried about you,' Sam said casually.

He was judging how much her clothes had cost and priced them beyond the salary of a working girl. Sheer nylons and high-heeled shoes, a bottle-green skirt and jacket over a white silk shirt. There was a feather set at a jaunty angle in her matching green hat and her handbag was soft crocodile skin. The whole outfit was new — and expensive. Irene Kline had moved up in the world since she'd left Felton Street.

She said, 'Oh!' like a startled fawn, adding quickly:

'Please tell her I'm all right. There's nothing to worry about. I couldn't write because — because I'm sworn to secrecy. But she mustn't worry and I'll see her soon.'

She was very happy. Her eyes shone and her face had a kind of radiance. Sam didn't want to spoil her illusions but there wasn't anything else he could do.

'Miss Kline,' he said sharply. 'Everything isn't all right and you've plenty to worry about. Take a look in your bedroom and you'll see what I mean.'

She was puzzled. She stepped past Sam to the open door of the bedroom. Her eyes opened as she saw the dead man; her face paled and the life seemed to go out of her. She started to sag at the knees and Sam had to support her.

'Is there any brandy in the house?' he asked.

She sat down on a chair, staring at the corpse, and nodded.

'In the cupboard, in the kitchen.'

Sam fetched the bottle and a glass. He poured a stiff drink and handed it to her. Irene gulped greedily and the colour came back to her cheeks. Her nerves steadied.

Sam wiped his prints off the bottle then the glass. The whole set-up smelled to him of a frame-up, and he wouldn't do Irene any good by being caught in the same trap.

'It's horrible,' she said, shuddering.

'Murder always is,' Sam agreed. 'It's the ultimate frustration of the individual.'

He lit two cigarettes, passed her one.

'I don't smoke,' she protested.

'Try it,' Sam advised. 'Good for the nerves.'

She placed the cigarette to her lips, puffed erratically, coughing. Sam decided it was time to ask questions. He gestured towards the dead man.

'His name's Bartlett. Ever see him before?'

Irene shook her head.

'No, he's a complete stranger. I can't imagine how he got here.' She paused. 'Was he killed — *here?*'

'It looks like it,' Sam said. 'How come you weren't home last night?'

She didn't want to answer that. Her lips shut in a tight line and her eyes clouded. Sam thought she was worrying more about someone else than herself; he hoped it wasn't Hugo Dare

'Look,' he said harshly, 'you're in a jam, Miss Kline. You've been deliberately framed for murder. A man is dead, in pyjamas, in your bed. Do you really believe a jury will take your word that you've never seen him? They'll call it a lover's quarrel and you'll take the rap . . . '

She coloured, looked at Sam appealingly.

'I can't say anything — I'm sworn to secrecy.'

Sam swore briefly. She sure was an innocent babe. Two years in San Francisco didn't seem to have taught her anything.

'Let's talk about Hugo Dare,' he said casually.

Irene nearly jumped out of her clothes.

'What do you know about Hugo?'

'Plenty,' Sam said grimly. 'I want to learn what *you* know.'

She said, in a low voice:

'He's a secret service agent working to catch a gang of spies. He asked me to help him by taking this bungalow. He said it would be a useful meeting place for his men; that's what happened last night — I went to a hotel while he met one of his agents.' She added, without noticing any irrelevancy: 'We're in love and he's going to marry me as soon as this job's finished.'

Sam felt suddenly weak. He gaped at her, asked in an incredulous tone: 'You really believe that stuff?'

'Of course!'

Sam nearly laughed. It was the funniest thing he'd ever heard; only it wasn't funny. It was tragic — for Irene.

He gripped her shoulders, shook her hard.

'Listen,' he said through gritted teeth. 'Hugo Dare is as crooked as they make 'em. He's the man behind a dozen rackets in this city; murder is nothing to him. He had Bartlett killed for some reason I don't know yet; then framed you to take the rap. He's going into politics; he can't afford to be associated with crime. That's why you've been framed. If the cops can pin it on you, Dare is sitting pretty. There won't even be an investigation.'

'That's absurd,' Irene replied, flushing. 'You don't understand — he loves me!'

'Look at it from the jury's point of view,' Sam urged. 'You're a hat check girl, not making much money — but you live in a ritzy bungalow and wear expensive clothes. They'll read one thing into that . . . '

'Hugo paid for everything,' Irene said. 'He told me it was necessary to play the part. There was nothing like that about it — he behaved like a gentleman.'

'Yeah,' Sam said bitterly. Dare wouldn't over-play his hand; why should he bother with a hat-check girl when he could buy all the glamour he wanted?

'But Dare will deny it all. He'll say he's never seen you. And the corpse will be scheduled as your lover — I'll bet this bungalow is even rented in Bartlett's name. This is the filthiest frame-up I've ever come across — and I've met a few.'

Irene smiled confidently.

'You're being very silly,' she scolded. 'Hugo will put everything right — I must see him at once.'

Sam crushed out his cigarette and put the butt in his pocket. If Irene wasn't going to help herself, his hands were tied. He wanted to get rid of the body, clean up the mess so the cops would find nothing — but that was no use if she wouldn't co-operate. He had to convince her that Dare was playing her for a sucker, and fast.

'Yeah,' he said, 'let's go see Hugo.'

'There's really no need for you to come,' Irene said. 'Hugo will take care of everything when I've told him what's happened.'

'That's what I'm afraid of. You may run into a little trouble. Anyway, my car's outside.'

They went out to the Ford. Sam didn't have to ask where Hugo Dare lived; his west side residence was famous. He tooled the car along Sloat Boulevard, travelling west to pick up Sky Line, turned south at the Fleishhaker Zoo. The Pacific was a vast expanse of blue on his right.

Sam said: 'How'd you come to meet Dare?'

Irene leaned back in the car, smiling. She seemed to have recovered from the shock of seeing a corpse on her bed; she was happy because she was going to see Hugo again.

'I met him at the 400 Club — I was the hat check girl there. A lot of men tried to get fresh, but I kept them off. Hugo used to come in regularly and he was always nice; he'd tip me and never tried to play around. I had to put up with a lot of insults from the male patrons, but Hugo always acted like a gentleman. He was kind of distinguished looking and — '

'Spare me the details,' Sam said. 'How come you fell for his smooth talk?'

Irene said, simply: 'I fell in love with him.'

There wasn't any answer to that so Sam drove in silence. After a while, Irene said:

'He met me after the Club closed one night and asked me to help him. That's when he told me he loved me and asked me to marry him.'

She sighed contentedly at the memory. 'Of course, when he told me he was in the secret service, I said I'd do anything to help. Then he asked me to move into the bungalow, as a screen he called it.'

Sam shook his head. How anyone could fall for that story was beyond him, but Irene was young and innocent — and she was in love. Now, she was in a jam, and if he didn't do something about it, she'd soon be frying on the hot seat. And Hugo Dare would get away with murder . . .

Dare's residence was a large, rambling house off to the left, between the Sky Line Boulevard and Lake Merced. Sam turned into the drive leading to the house. The drive wound between close-grown trees, screened from view; sand dunes separated it from the nearest neighbours. It was splendidly isolated and that would suit Dare, a man who doubtless had many strange callers.

The house was set on a small hill, surrounded by well-kept lawns dotted with flowering evergreens and statuettes. The porch opened onto a wide verandah with trailing vines; French windows glittered in the sunlight. Sam parked the Ford and helped Irene out.

'I'll see him alone,' she said. 'There's no need for you to come in, really there isn't.'

She had the bubbling over-confidence of a maiden in love. She lived in a world of her own, untouched by harsh reality — but it wasn't going to last. Not for long.

Sam sauntered to the steps, taking his time. Irene ran ahead, eager to see the man she loved. Sam watched her pull the bell-chain, saw the door open and a uniformed butler appear.

She said: 'Irene Kline to see Hugo Dare.'

She would have gone in, but the butler blocked her off.

'Mr. Dare is busy,' he said firmly. 'I can't disturb him.'

Irene stammered: 'It's important. If you

give him my name, I'm sure he'll see me.'

The butler eyed her coldly, not budging an inch.

'Mr. Dare gave instructions that he was not to be disturbed.'

Irene hesitated, not knowing what to do. Sam did. He moved easily up the steps, grey eyes smiling. He reached the door, leaned on it with his full weight. The butler gasped and gave ground as the door opened under pressure. Sam took Irene's arm and carried her in with him.

'Mr. Dare is going to be disturbed,' he drawled. 'This young lady has business with him. She's going to marry him — didn't Hugo tell you?'

Irene missed his sarcasm, but the butler didn't. He looked at Sam woodenly.

'Mr. Dare isn't going to like this.'

Sam touched his shoulder holster significantly.

'Too bad. Lead the way to Hugo — and don't stop to talk to anyone on the way. I'm allergic to company.'

The butler shrugged, turned to pad softly down a carpeted passage. Irene followed, her head in the air. She still didn't know something was wrong; she believed in Hugo. Sam brought up the rear. He loosened his Luger in its holster; he didn't think Dare would start a shooting match on his own doorstep, but he wasn't taking chances.

They covered a tiled hall. A wide staircase swept upwards in a graceful curve; at the top, another carpeted passage led to double oak doors. The butler knocked, announced:

'Miss Kline — and a man.'

He would have withdrawn, but Sam pushed him into the room ahead of him. He wanted the butler where he could keep an eye on him; he didn't want him running for help. The room was large and beautifully furnished; red drapes covered the walls, a thick pile extended to the fireplace. Electric bulbs hung from a crystal chandelier and Hugo Dare sat on a well-cushioned divan.

Dare wasn't alone on the divan; he had a blonde with him. That stopped Irene cold; she hadn't expected to find Hugo with another woman. Her face went pale.

Sam moved into the room behind the

butler, watching Dare and the blonde. Hugo came to his feet, wiping lipstick from his face. He stared at Sam and said, gently:

'Mr. Spain, isn't it? I'm sorry to see you here.'

Sam didn't bother to reply. He was weighing Dare against other crooks he had known. The man was tall, over six foot, and broad with it. His suit was tailored, expensive. His silver-grey hair had an artificial wave which gave him a distinguished air. He was lantern-jawed, with black, piercing eyes.

Irene went towards him, holding out her hands uncertainly.

'Something horrible happened at the bungalow,' she started. 'A man — '

Dare cut in coldly, nodding towards Irene.

'Who's your girl friend, Spain?'

Sam's grey eyes were bleak. He said, flatly:

'She seems to think you're in love with her, that you're going to marry her.'

It was the blonde on the divan who laughed. She lay back in the cushions, lazily brushing her platinum hair. Her body was covered by a crimson gown stretched so tight it looked like a second skin. It was backless and cut low in front.

Irene seemed scared to look at the blonde. Her eyes turned appealingly on Dare.

'Hugo,' she said, 'who is this girl?'

Hugo Dare dropped on to the divan. The blonde's dress was slit from hem to thigh, and she stretched a silk-clad leg with careless abandon.

'Paula,' he said, watching Irene. 'She's a friend of mine — if it's any of your business.'

Paula kissed Hugo.

'I wonder why she should think you're going to marry her?' she murmured, laughing.

'I can't imagine,' Dare replied casually. 'I've never seen her before!'

Sam felt sorry for Irene. She held herself stiffly, her face white. She was having difficulty in grasping what was going on around her.

Sam said: 'She was hat check girl at the 400 Club. Remember now?'

Hugo Dare looked at Irene with interest. He might have been inspecting a squashed slug through a microscope.

'That's nice for her,' he said politely. 'I use the 400 occasionally — I might have seen her around. What of it?'

Paula came off the divan in a slinky, gliding movement. She swayed across the room, swinging her hips. She slapped Irene across the face, grated:

'Get out you cheap little no-good! I've seen your sort before. I know what you're after — you're in trouble and you think you can make Hugo pay blackmail. Get out before I scratch your eyes out!'

'Now, Paula,' Dare said soothingly. 'I'm sure this unfortunate girl will leave without giving trouble.' He swung round, directing his speech at Sam.

'I suggest you take your friend away. You're interrupting something.'

Irene pleaded with Hugo.

'You promised me — '

Dare laughed in her face. His tone changed, became harder.

'You'd better leave. I've never seen you before and you can't prove I have. As if

I'd be interested in a hat check girl — when I've got Paula! Perhaps Spain will marry you!'

Irene recoiled as if she'd been struck. Tears welled up in her eyes. She began to quiver.

Dare said, brutally: 'You're not even pretty. I wouldn't date you for one evening, you slut!'

Irene moaned: 'I love you, Hugo. If it's secret service business that's — '

Paula jeered: 'Secret service! She's out of her mind!'

Dare said: 'Poor girl, she's wandering. Take her to see a psychiatrist, Spain, perhaps he can help her. And do try to impress on her that I've never seen her before, that she means nothing to me.' He repeated, with emphasis: 'Absolutely nothing.'

Paula laughed harshly and went back to the divan. She stretched her supple body and called to Dare:

'I'm lonely, Hugo. Get rid of these people.'

Irene was crying, her hands clenched tightly. She tried to beat Dare's chest with her hands.

'You said you loved me — you — '

Hugo Dare raised his hand and struck her across the face. He laughed again.

'Love you? You poor sap — if I wanted you, I'd take you. But I don't. I can't imagine any man wanting you!'

Paula said, from the divan:

'That's it, Hugo, tell her.' She smoothed out the cushions. 'Come and kiss me again, darling.'

Sam tapped Irene on the shoulder.

'Let's go,' he said. 'If I see any more I'll break into tears myself.' He turned to Dare, said flatly: 'Enjoy yourself, Hugo — you haven't much time.'

Dare smiled coldly. His voice was a chilling whisper.

'I'd advise you to stay out of this affair, Spain.'

Sam turned his back on him. He prodded the butler in the ribs.

'You walk in front,' he grunted.

The butler went out of the room. Sam gripped Irene's arm tightly and followed. The last sound he heard was Dare's careless laughter as he moved across to the blonde on the divan. They went down the stairs, across the hall to the front porch.

The butler watched them go down the steps, along the drive to a battered Ford. Sam had his hands full with Irene; she walked as if she were drugged. Sluggishly, her shoulders slumped forward, tears streaming silently down her face. She didn't make a sound as she cried.

Sam helped her into the seat, slid behind the driving wheel and started the car. He drove fast, out through the open gates on to Sky Line. Dare would move fast now that he knew Irene had help; Sam wanted to beat him to the next move. He shot a sideways glance at Irene. She held her face between shaking hands, crying soundlessly. Her whole body shook and quivered. Something had died inside her; her beautiful dream-world had been brutally shattered and she was all alone in the ruins.

Sam said: 'We're going back to the bungalow. I'm going to get rid of the body. I want you to clear up the mess. When the police arrive, they'll be nothing for them. Understand?'

Irene didn't move, didn't say anything. She stared blindly at the windscreen, not seeing anything. Sam cursed. He eased his foot off the accelerator and shook her roughly.

'Listen, Irene. We're going back to the bungalow. There's a dead man on your bed, remember?'

She nodded dully. Her voice was a monotone, without sparkle.

'I'll do anything you say.'

Sam felt relief surge through him. They were the first words she'd spoken since Dare hit her. She was with him. Sam tried to be gentle with her, but time was against them.

'You've had an unpleasant experience,' he said softly, 'but you'll get over it. Remember that, you *will* get over it. You must do everything I tell you, that way I'll get you out of this mess. I'm your friend, Irene — you can rely on me.'

She tried to smile, but the result wasn't anything to shout about. Sam concentrated on his driving. Irene was a sack of limp rags beside him. He swung the Ford to the right to pick up Sloat Boulevard, right again down Meadowbrook Drive, then left into Eucalyptus Drive.

He cut the Ford's speed as he approached 212, cruising easily. He didn't want to attract attention. He picked out the green-tiled bungalow, behind poplar and spruce, and the place had an air of activity about it.

Sam didn't like that. He liked it even less when he saw the two police cars standing outside.

4

Sam Spain kept right on, going past the
bungalow, till he picked up Nineteenth
Avenue. He swung the Ford left and
headed north, past the Carl Larsen Park,
crossing Taraval and Ortega.

His head was in a whirl. Dare hadn't
had time to get the cops to Eucalyptus
Drive ahead of him, so Muir must be
working with the gangster-politician.
Ambrose Muir must have 'phoned the
police immediately after Sam had left the
400 Club; he'd contacted Hugo Dare too,
that's how the lantern-jawed man had
known Sam's name. Sam smiled grimly;
he'd learnt something from that. He
could get at Dare through the night club
manager.

The Ford passed Irving and Lincoln
Way and slanted into Golden Gate Park.
Sam glanced back; there was no sign of
pursuit. For the time being, they were
safe; but he had to get Irene under cover,

51

and fast. Her flaming red hair was too conspicuous for her to remain in the open.

He parked the car on the grass verge of a hill. If anyone noticed them, they were just a man and a girl parking, and maybe petting; nothing suspicious in that. Below them, Stow Lake wound across the park; looking west, beyond the stadium, the waters of the Pacific glittered blue and silver in the sun. It was a pleasant spot.

Sam unfastened the dashboard locker and brought out a whisky flask. He handed it to Irene.

'Take a slug,' he said. 'You need it.'

She obeyed automatically, tilting the flask to her lips, coughing as the raw spirit burned her throat. Sam lit a cigarette.

'Do something about your face,' Sam said. 'You look like a cyclone hit you.'

She fished in her handbag, the one with soft crocodile skin Dare had bought her. She wiped her face and used lipstick and powder. She looked a hundred per cent. better.

'He said he loved me,' she moaned softly. 'We were going to be married.'

Sam said, brutally: 'Cut that out! You know now what sort of man Hugo Dare is — forget him. You've other worries . . . '

She straightened up, nodded, trying to get a grip on herself.

'What am I going to do? You'll help me, won't you, Mr. Spain?'

Sam nodded.

'I'll do what I can, but you must follow orders. First, Dare won't stop till he's pinned this murder rap on you. He can't afford to. If the cops catch you, you'll be framed. Judge and jury will be against you. You haven't a chance.'

He paused, drew on his cigarette, staring across the swell of grass to silver pines. The sun was warm and Sam's stomach informed him that he'd missed lunch.

'If you try to leave San Francisco, you'll be picked up for sure. Same at my place, or your mother's. You've got to hide out somewhere till I've had a chance to clear you — that means pinning murder on Hugo Dare and that isn't going to be easy.'

He considered it silently, then said:

'Dare wouldn't have killed Bartlett himself. He'd hire a man for the job. I've got to find that man and make him talk — it's the only way.'

Irene was becoming conscious of her position.

'Where will I go?' she wanted to know. 'I don't know anywhere I can hide.'

Sam's breath hissed in sudden intake as a cop on a motor-cycle came along the road. Sam pulled Irene to him and put his arms about her.

'This is just an innocent petting session, understand?'

He kissed her, hardly tasting her lips for wondering if the policeman would stop. He hugged Irene's slim form tighter, kissed her again. He heard the motor-cycle stop.

'Break it up,' a voice said.

Sam turned, protested: 'Aw, can't a guy kiss his girl without you mugs interferring?'

The cop grinned broadly.

'Sorry pal,' he said. 'No parking on the grass. There's a parking lot down the road, by the tea gardens.' He looked at

Irene. 'Wouldn't mind being in your shoes myself,' he grunted, turning back to his machine.

Sam released Irene. She straightened her jacket while Sam wiped lipstick off his mouth. He grinned at her.

'I could have enjoyed that,' he said, 'under more favourable conditions!'

She lowered her eyes, said nothing. Sam watched the cop ride off, started the Ford and drove in the opposite direction.

'Now you have a taste of what it's like to be hunted,' Sam told her grimly. 'Always ducking for cover, afraid you'll be recognized, never feeling safe. Lucky for us that cop wasn't suspicious.'

He drove out of the park, up Fell Street and travelled east.

'Where are we going?' Irene asked in a troubled voice.

'Friend of mine keeps a café down by the waterfront. He'll hide you for the present.'

The Ford crossed Market Street and turned down 10th. East of Third Street, the houses were jammed together in poverty and squalor. There was a smell of fish and laundries mixed up with railroad smoke and cheap cooking from dingy cafés.

'Not the most select area,' Sam commented, 'but you'll be safe with Joey. I'd trust my life to that guy.'

Irene said: 'I'm making trouble for you, Mr. Spain. Hadn't you better leave me? I'll get away somehow.'

'Not on your life — I thrive on trouble. Especially when it's dished out by rats like Hugo Dare. And call me Sam.'

Joey's café was right on the waterfront, overlooking the bay. There was a view of the docks, jammed with all kinds of ships, coal barges, tankers, fishing boats. The San Francisco-Oakland Bay Bridge stretched steel cables across the water, a man-made highway busy with east-bound traffic.

Sam drove his car into the yard behind Joey's café. He climbed out, looked around. There was no-one to see them. He hurried Irene through the back door, into a dirty, smelly kitchen.

'Hi, Joey, I've brought you a visitor,' he said to the short, fat man reading the sporting page of a newspaper. 'Someone who doesn't want callers, cops or otherwise.'

Joey looked up. His bald head shone like polished ivory and he waggled bushy eyebrows as he looked at Irene. He got up, held out his hand to the girl. His thick lips moved in speech.

'You'll be safe here, miss. Any friend of Sam's is a friend of mine.'

He led the way through a damp passage, the paper flaking off the walls. A bare, uncarpeted stairway led to a tiny room with a shuttered window, a bed, a chair and a washstand. It was clean but not elegant.

'Sorry, I've nothing better, miss,' Joey said apologetically, 'but you'll be safe enough here.' He looked at Sam. 'You don't have to tell me anything, but — '

Sam smiled with his eyes. He lit a cigarette, said:

'Irene's been framed for murder by Hugo Dare. She's got to stay under cover till I can clear her. That may take a little time.'

Joey nodded.

'It's time somebody put the skids under Dare.'

'I'm afraid this is awkward for you, Joey,' Irene said.

The fat man laughed.

'Sam saved my life one time. I know what it's like to be threatened by mobsters. I'd help anyone in trouble and there isn't anything I wouldn't do for Sam. You don't have to worry about me, miss — I'm glad of the chance to hit back at the crooks who spoil this city.'

Sam said: 'I'm hungry, Joey. Fix some lunch. I've a little shopping to do, but I'll be back soon. Irene, don't move out of this room and don't show your face at the window.'

He went down the stairs and out onto the waterfront. He left his car in the yard, walked down back-streets. He found the shop he wanted and made his purchases. When he returned to the café, he had a parcel under his arm.

Joey had a meal waiting and Sam and Irene ate together, in her room. The girl seemed to have lost her appetite but Sam ate enough for both of them. When the plates had been cleared away, Sam turned to Irene. He said:

'You'll find a complete change of clothes in the parcel. Irene Kline disappears and Flossie Smith is born. But we've got to fix that hair first.'

He borrowed a pair of scissors from Joey, draped a sheet round Irene's shoulders.

'I'm sorry about this,' he said. 'It's necessary.'

'I don't mind,' she said. 'Nothing seems to matter any more.'

She sat in silence while Sam snipped with the scissors. He trimmed her red hair to a short, rather ragged bob, then mixed a black dye he had bought. When he'd finished, she looked quite different.

'I'll wait downstairs while you change,' he told her. 'Parcel up your clothes and I'll lose them somewhere.'

She was only ten minutes. Sam viewed her with approval. Her stockings were cheap cotton; a baggy black skirt hung from her waist; a soiled blouse and down-at-heel shoes completed her dress. With short, black hair, Sam didn't think anyone would recognize her at a casual glance. And he didn't intend anyone to get a close-up.

'I've arranged for you to work in the kitchen. That'll account for your living here,' Sam said. 'Don't go out. Avoid contact with the customers. When you're not working in the kitchen, stay in this room, out of sight. And don't worry — I'll be working to clear you of this murder rap.'

'My mother,' Irene said wistfully. 'I'd like to see her.'

Sam shook his head.

'Too risky. The cops will be watching her. I'll tell her you're safe — and stop thinking about Hugo. He's not worth your wasting time over.'

Her face drained of blood and she began to shake again.

'He called me a slut. He said he didn't want me, that no man could want me — '

Sam kissed her quickly.

'Maybe one man wants you,' he said softly. 'We'll talk about that later.'

He made a parcel of her hair clippings, collected her clothes and the empty dye bottle. He wasn't leaving anything around for prying eyes to see. The whole lot would go to the bottom of the bay.

Downstairs, he said to Joey:

'Keep an eye on her; she's too upset to know what she's doing. I shall keep clear of this place. Give me a ring if anything goes wrong. If I don't hear from you, I'll assume everything's fine.'

Joey stroked his bald head.

'Okay, Sam. They'll get the girl over my dead body.'

Sam grinned.

'I wouldn't want that to happen, Joey. Even a private eye likes to have a few friends!'

He went out to the yard. Darkness crept over the bay; the last rays of the setting sun shot blood-red lances across deserted wharves. Sam drove the Ford north, along the waterfront, glad of the wisps of seamist drifting inland. He waited till he came to a bleak stretch of foreshore, till the fog eddied protective shrouds about him, then he stopped the car.

He carried the bundle of Irene's clothes and hair, the black dye bottle, to the edge of the jetty, weighted them, threw them into the swirling waters. They sank downward, leaving a trail of air-bubbles that quickly dispersed. Sam turned away; Irene had a chance now.

He started the Ford again, headed along 17th Street to Franklin Square, turned right and pulled up outside the Alameda Hotel. He went in through the tiled hallway to the desk.

'Mrs. Kline,' he said to the clerk. 'She's staying here. I'd like to see her.'

The clerk, a sharp-eyed youngster with a cleft chin, looked at Sam suspiciously. He couldn't think of any reason why Sam shouldn't call on one of the hotel's guests, so he said:

'She's in. Room 317, third floor.'

Sam said: 'Thanks,' and crossed to the elevator. It was self-operated and Sam let himself out on the third floor. He walked the passage, reading door numbers. He knocked on 317.

Mrs. Kline opened the door. Sam went in, looked round quickly.

'Have the police been here?' he asked.

Mrs. Kline was startled.

'Why, no.' She paused. 'Is Irene in some kind of trouble?'

Sam told her about Hugo Dare, about the corpse on the bed at 212 Eucalyptus Drive, about the scene at Dare's house.

'Irene's safe for the time being,' he finished. 'She's hiding out with a friend of mine.'

He didn't say where; he thought the fewer people who knew where Irene was the better. Mrs. Kline said:

'I must go to her. My poor daughter — that horrible man. The police — '

Sam shook his head.

'You can't see her till this business is over. The police follow orders — and those orders come from Dare. He's got plenty of pull in this city and he's determined to pin the murder on Irene. She's got to stay under cover until I can clear her.'

Mrs. Kline nodded.

'Whatever you say, Mr. Spain. I only want to help Irene.'

'The best way you can help her is to go back to Paradise Valley and keep your mouth shut. You'll get a visit from the cops. If you can hint she's hiding out in the vicinity — without saying as much

— that'll help draw their attention off the track. And don't worry. I'm going after Hugo Dare and I won't stop till he's on trial for his life.'

Mrs. Kline said:

'I'm very grateful to you, Mr. Spain. I don't have much money but — '

Sam shook his head.

'Don't worry about that. I don't like to see an innocent girl go to the chair and a rat like Dare get away with it.'

He left, went down the elevator. The sharp-eyed clerk watched him, said nothing. Sam climbed into the Ford and drove up Bryant Street to the Embarcadero. He swung north and followed the curve of the bay.

Sam remembered an address. 11a Commercial Street. Clint Bartlett's address. He badly wanted to know something about the dead man on Irene's bed and he thought a visit to Commercial Street might help.

He passed under the San Francisco-Oakland Bay Bridge and drove on to the Ferry Building at the foot of Market Street. Commercial Street was off to the left, a straight road between drab apartment blocks leading through China-town. Sam remembered the package of heroin powder he'd found on Bartlett; that argued a close connection with Chinatown, even though 11a was outside the yellow section proper.

Sam parked his car in an alley and proceeded on foot. 11a was the basement of a disused store. Sam idled past, watching for some sign of habitation. He saw nothing to arouse his suspicions. The fog screened him from the few people about as he slipped down the area steps to the front door.

The door was locked but that didn't stop him for long. He worked on the lock with a piece of flexible steel wire, listening for the clicking of the tumblers. He drew on thin suede gloves and opened the door. It was pitch black and silent as a grave inside.

Sam gently closed the door behind him, stood motionless, waiting, listening. No movement came from the darkness around him. He switched on a pocket torch, flashed it round. He found the window and drew the curtain across.

Then he searched the room.

There was nothing much to it. Bartlett had been a man of spartan habits. The bed was a network of wire springs with a double blanket across. His food seemed to consist of whisky and bread and cheese. His clothes were few and dirty.

Sam went through the room carefully, wondering why Hugo Dare had killed this man. There were no letters, papers of any kind. Sam went through the cupboard, tore up a loose floorboard to discover a nest of spiders, tipped out the blankets. Nothing, nothing at all to give him a lead.

The pockets of the suit hanging in the closet revealed a pen-knife, a few coins, cigarettes, another package of heroin. Sam felt round the lining. Again, nothing. He shoved the things back, and his fingers caught on a tear in the pocket lining. He groped inside, pulled out a folded paper.

There was an address on it: Wang Lee, House of the Seven Moons, Pagoda Place.

Sam memorized the address, put the paper back. Wang Lee might have nothing to do with Bartlett's death but Sam was going to call at the House of the Seven Moons. He left the room, locking the door behind him, and went up the area steps. He pulled off his suede gloves.

The fog was thicker now. It came in from the bay in gusty clouds of damp mist, smelling of brine. Sam groped his way to the alley where he'd left his car. He didn't see the two men waiting for him in the shadows.

They came at him from behind and a sap glanced the side of his head, sending him reeling, half-stunned. Strong hands grabbed his arms, twisted them behind him. The other man slammed a fistful of brass knuckle-duster into Sam's mouth. Sam spat out blood and a loose tooth, coughing.

The fist came again, bringing sharp pain to Sam's face. He fell forward, dragging the man who held him to the ground. It was too dark to see his attackers and they said nothing. Sam lashed out with his foot. A hand caught his ankle, turned it. Fists drummed into his stomach, filling him with a nauseating sickness. A boot crashed against his skull and bright lights flickered through the fog.

Sam retched, tried to crawl away, groping for his Luger. He got it half out of the holster, then it was torn from his grasp. He heard the gun clatter metallically on the cobblestones.

One of his attackers must be a large, strong man; he lifted Sam like a baby, held him in a grip of iron while the other man beat him viciously. The knuckle-dusters scraped the skin off Sam's face, bringing tears to his eyes. Sam tore one arm free, swung it wildly. It connected with something soft and the man with the knuckle-dusters moaned. The large man cursed briefly and began to twist Sam's arm.

Sam hacked his shin, rolling free. He hit the ground in a heap and went after the Luger. He could see the blue metallic shine winking at him through the fog. A heavy boot stamped on his hand and he cried out in sudden agony; another boot kicked the gun away from him.

Sam tried to get up, but they wouldn't let him. Two pairs of boots battered his body; his ribs ached and he tried to protect his face with his hands. They kicked him low down, in the pit of the stomach.

They went on kicking him till a red haze appeared before his eyes and a noise like Niagara pounded in his eardrums. Sam went limp; his muscles wouldn't function properly and he couldn't crawl away from the ceaseless barrage of heavy boots.

A black veil dropped across him, a blanket of darkness and agonizing pain. A pair of large hands dragged him upright and the man with knuckle-dusters hit him in the mouth, again and again. Sam wasn't feeling much now . . . he sagged at the knees, almost unconscious. A voice said:

'Keep out of the Bartlett case, Spain. Next time — '

Sam fell into a black tunnel where time ceased to exist.

5

He felt as if he might have been cast up on a beach after being in the sea for a long time. Only no beach had hard cobblestones and no waves could have given his body such a battering. He was cold and damp; that was due to the fog which eddied and swirled about him.

Sam Spain began to remember things again. He straightened out, trying his arms and legs one by one. No bones seemed to be broken, but it cost him a lot of effort to stand up. He leaned against the Ford, gulping down air. His face was a mask of dried blood; his hands and shirt front were matted with the stuff.

He opened the car door, fumbled in the dashboard locker for his whisky flask. He unscrewed the cap, raised the bottle to his lips. He took a swig, rinsed his mouth, spat it out. His tongue, feeling round the roof of his mouth, told him he'd lost two front teeth.

He raised the flask again, poured the raw spirit down his throat. It burned, and he felt better. He sat in the driving seat, relaxing with a cigarette. The weed soothed his nerves. After a while, he switched on his flashlight and went searching for his Luger. He never found it; his attackers had taken it with them.

Sam started the Ford and turned out of Commercial Street, into Market Street. He headed south-west driving slowly and carefully because San Francisco's main thoroughfare was busy with traffic and Sam's reactions were slow. He passed 10th and Van Ness, but didn't stop at his office. He turned right, into Brady Street where he had a room in an apartment house.

Leaving his car at the curbside, Sam went through the porch and up the stairs. He was glad his room was on the first floor, glad he didn't have to climb any more stairs. He fitted his key into the lock, but he needn't have bothered; the door was unlocked and the light on.

Sam went in, recognising the tall, lanky man sprawled in his best chair.

71

'You look like you ran into trouble,' Lieutenant Ernst said quietly.

Sam nodded, trying to keep his tone light.

'Walked into a lamp-post in the fog,' he said.

Ernst made no comment. He watched Sam go through to the bathroom and start running water. He levered himself out of the chair and followed.

Sam ignored him, bathed his face, used astringent and sticking plaster. He went into the bedroom and selected a clean shirt and suit; he didn't like walking round covered in blood. Ernst lit two cigarettes, passed one to Sam.

He was over six foot and so thin that every woman he met wanted to marry him and feed him up. He had a swarthy face and tiny, bright eyes. His suit was too large for him, a ready-made suit that hung in folds about his skeleton frame. He looked brittle, as if he would snap at the lightest touch, but Sam knew he was plenty tough. A cop on the Homicide Detail has to be.

Ernst said, quietly:

'Where's the girl?'

Sam said: 'Which girl?'

Ernst snapped the brim of his hat carelessly.

'Redhead, Irene Kline. You drove her out to Hugo Dare's place.'

Sam looked at Ernst. He had worked with the lieutenant when he'd been in the force; he knew that Ernst was an honest cop. But honest cops have to carry out orders too; and Dare would be pulling strings from his political stronghold. Sam decided he couldn't take the lieutenant into his confidence.

'Oh, Miss Kline,' he said casually. 'I guess she's on her way back to Paradise Valley.'

'What makes you think that?'

Sam shrugged.

'Mrs. Kline hired me to find her daughter. I did. Now I guess they've both gone home. San Francisco is no place for a girl who doesn't know her way around.'

Ernst's voice was very quiet, very penetrating.

'Where'd you find her, Sam?'

Sam had finished dressing. He brought

a bottle of whisky from the closet, located a couple of tumblers. He filled them, handed the lieutenant one.

'Funny thing,' he said. 'I was driving along Market Street and there she was, on the sidewalk. I hailed her, drove her to Dare's place at her request. Afterwards, I set her down at the railroad and told her to go back to Nevada. I guess she did.'

Sam stretched himself out on the bed, alternately sipping from the tumbler and smoking a cigarette. Ernst drew up a chair, sat astride it, his face close to Sam's. He made a clicking noise with his teeth.

'You wouldn't know anything about a dead man in Eucalyptus Drive? You wouldn't know that he was found in the bungalow Irene Kline had been using? You wouldn't know anything about those things, would you, Sam?'

'That's right,' Sam agreed, 'I wouldn't!'

Ernst sighed, and shook his head sadly.

'I don't know why, but the D.A.'s excited about this case. It has to be sewn up in a hurry. I guess somebody's putting pressure on him. I want the girl, Sam.'

'Warrant out for her?'

'Not yet, Sam. Any time though. The dead man was in pyjamas, in her bed. I guess they were more than acquaintances — the set-up looks like a love-nest. They quarrelled and she stabbed him. It fits.'

'Yeah,' Sam said bitterly, 'it fits so good it smells! Why would anyone put on pressure to bring a girl who killed her lover? What's so important about that, lieutenant? Go on, tell me.'

Ernst rose to his feet. He finished his drink and wandered to the door. He paused, said:

'I hate to see you get mixed up in a thing like this, Sam. Leave it alone. And don't walk into any more lamp-posts!'

He went out, pulling down the snap brim of his hat.

Sam watched the clock for a while, resting and thinking. It was a little after nine-thirty and he'd had a busy day; but it wasn't over yet. He wanted to see Wang Lee; then it might not be a bad idea to drop in at the 400 Club and chat awhile with Trixy. That girl liked money and she might have information to sell, the sort of information that would help send Hugo Dare to the hot seat.

He collected a new gun, a Detective Special, and fitted a clip of .38 slugs. It made a comforting bulge in the holster under his jacket. He went down the stairs, out to his car.

Sam eased the Ford into the north-west bound traffic on Market Street and kept going, past Leavenworth and Powell Streets to Grant Avenue. He turned left, heading north for Chinatown.

Crossing Bush Street, he hit the yellow section. Chop-suey joints mingled with tourist shops and the sidewalks were alive with sight-seers. Chinatown extended as far as Columbus Avenue, branching right and left of the main thoroughfare. Sam turned off Grant, left along Sacremento Street, right into Pagodo Place.

It wasn't a select area. Too many unwashed Chinese lived too close together. There was a smell from the dark alleys and shadows moved like fleeting wraiths. Tourists didn't leave the lighted streets after dark; this was the real Chinatown.

Sam found the House of the Seven

Moons without any trouble. The house was large, isolated from overcrowded tenements by narrow, twisting alleys. It was an old house, well-built, but with the outside allowed to decay. Inside, you might find an oriental palace or a slum; you couldn't tell till you got there.

Sam locked the car doors and climbed the stone steps to the house. There weren't any lights and the windows looked as if they were boarded up on the inside. Sam crashed the rusty iron knocker three times, sending hollow echoes far into the house. He waited.

He waited a long time, knocked again, sending a rat scuttling into the shadowed area below the steps. He heard no footsteps and the door opened silently. A yellow face looked out impassively. A flat voice said:

'Go away.'

Sam stuck his foot in the door. He handed the servant a business card, scrawled the name: Bartlett, on it.

'I want to see Wang Lee,' Sam said. 'Tell him I'll stay right here till he does see me.'

A yellow claw seized the card and retreated. The door shut in Sam's face. He waited again. He got tired of waiting and used the knocker again. There were shadows across the street, shadows that moved, and Sam figured he was too conspicuous a target where he was.

The door opened and the servant beckoned him in. No words were wasted. Inside the House of the Seven Moons, it was dark as a closed box. Sam had to hold the trailing housecoat of the Chinese to follow him. They went up a short flight of stairs, along a passage down steps, turning right, left and right again.

Sam couldn't see a thing; he had to trust the man he was following. More stairs, up and down again. More turns to right and left. They might have completed a circle and Sam wouldn't have known.

At the end of a short passage, the servant opened a door. Sam went through into a lighted room. The door closed behind him and he was alone with Wang Lee.

The room was luxuriously furnished in oriental style. Incense pervaded the air.

There were no windows and drapes covered the walls. Wang Lee sat behind a carved desk, idly playing with exquisite jade pieces.

'The Honourable Spain desires audience with his humble servant?' said Wang Lee gravely.

Sam's grey eyes smiled. Wang Lee spoke without the slightest trace of an accent; he was an educated man, playing the part of the traditionally over-polite Chinese. It was a game two could play.

'If the most venerable Wang Lee pleases,' he replied.

Wang Lee smiled and the two men studied one another in silence. Wang Lee was dressed in silk robes of bright blue with a scarlet dragon embroidered across the chest; a skull cap hid his hair; the toes of his slippers were curved. He was a slender man, a little taller than Sam. His face was an ivory mask, revealing no trace of emotion; his waxed moustache was long and hung in an inverted-U. He had let his finger nails grow to the length of three inches and they were sharply pointed and painted scarlet.

'What is it the Master of Spies requires of his trembling servant?' Wang Lee asked.

'O Celestial One,' Sam replied, 'this unworthy clod of earth is seeking wisdom.'

Wang Lee bowed.

'Even the lowliest of the Earth seek the Truth in all matters.'

'Such wisdom is attainable by only the most high-born mortals,' Sam said graciously. 'So it is to the omniscient Wang Lee that this humble worm must crawl.'

Wang Lee toyed with a jade piece. He said softly:

'And this wisdom the Prince of Detectives seeks? In what way shall the servant beg to instruct his master?'

Sam forgot to play-act. He leaned forward, tense, his lips forming a harsh line.

'A man named Bartlett, a heroin addict, has been murdered. I want to know something about him. Who he was, how he lived — and why he was killed.'

Wang Lee smiled faintly.

'The King of Investigators mocks this unworthy slave. It pleases him to pretend that all is not known to him. The ignorance of the despicable Wang Lee is profound; he knows neither why the unfortunate Bartlett was sent to join his ancestors, nor why the Emperor of Finders-out should assume the unbecoming mantle of ignorance.'

Sam tried another tack.

'Perhaps the wise and all-knowing Wang Lee can tell this worthless servant where the ill-fated Bartlett obtained a supply of heroin?'

'The Dust of Dreams is not for those lawful slaves who worship at the feet of Uncle Sam. The honest Wang Lee does not regret his lack of knowledge in the ways of the criminal; in this case, the absence of knowledge is profound wisdom.'

'Then why is it,' Sam asked softly, 'that the dead man had your name and address in his pocket?'

Wang Lee shrugged.

'Truly the ways of men are strange. That the abode of this lowly worm should be known to the late friend of the

All-seeing Eye is inexplicable.'

Sam said: 'He was no friend of mine. The first time I saw him he was wearing an ice-pick in his heart.'

'The user of Dream Dust will dream forever,' Wang Lee commented.

Sam rose from his seat. Wang Lee wasn't giving anything away and any further conversation would be a waste of time. But he had the idea Wang Lee knew something if he could find the lever to open his mouth.

'Perhaps I shall call on the Omnipotent One again,' Sam said.

Wang Lee rose too. He bowed.

'That pleasure is one for which I shall offer prayer, O Terror of Lawbreakers.'

There was a lot more to it, reams of polite hogwash, then Wang Lee summoned his servant and Sam followed him through endless dark passages that wound up and down stairs, to the front door. He breathed a sigh of relief as he stood on the sidewalk outside the House of the Seven Moons again.

A clock struck the half hour after ten. The 400 Club would be livening up; it would be a good time to see Trixy again. Sam unlocked the car doors and settled behind the driving wheel of the Ford.

The fog swirled about him as he drove along Clay Street, out of Chinatown. He picked up speed on Van Ness and headed north. Maybe it was Wang Lee who had supplied Bartlett with heroin; that would account for his foxy behaviour. And Sam knew that the Narcotics Detail were working overtime on a sudden influx of drugs into San Francisco.

At the top of Van Ness, he swung left onto Marina Boulevard. Nobody moved outside the 400 Club; it was opposite the Marina Park and shrouded in mist. Sam parked his car and walked towards the sound of a swing band.

Inside, the night club had plenty of glitter. The tables were crowded and dancers packed the parquet strip. He saw Trixy moving between the tables. She was wearing something scanty and selling chocolates and cigarettes. Sam waved her into a corner.

The blonde looked around, to make sure that Muir or his stooges weren't watching her. Sam pushed a dollar bill into her hand.

'You may be able to help me again,' he said.

She was worried about something.

'Not here,' she said quickly. 'In ten minutes, in the dressing room.'

Sam nodded. He crossed to the bar and bought a drink. Sipping it, he looked round the club. Trixy was working her way to the back of the club; Muir looked out from the archway, scanning the crowd. He had Cabot at his side. Both men disappeared in the direction of Muir's office.

The dance ended and the lights dimmed. The cabaret began. Eight lovely girls in the minimum of clothing pranced onto the parquet. Spotlights gleamed on bare legs and shoulders and the male patrons applauded.

Sam slipped between the tables, making his way to the arch back of the club. With the lights dimmed and attention rivetted on the dancing girls, he didn't think anyone would notice him. Trixy had timed it nicely; with the girls on-stage, the dressing room would be empty.

He passed Muir's office. The door was shut and the mumble of voices too blurred for Sam to hear what was said. He went to the dressing room and found the blonde waiting for him.

'Muir asked a lot of questions after you left,' she said. 'He's got the idea somebody talked about Irene. I'm scared.'

'He won't know it was you who put me onto her,' Sam said encouragingly. He folded another dollar bill, passed it to her.

'I don't like it,' Trixy grumbled. 'Muir's a dangerous man.'

'All I want is to know if a man named Bartlett ever used the club. He was a short, thick-set man and the pupils of his eyes would be tiny, like pinpoints. He was a heroin addict.'

Trixy shook her blonde curls.

'I haven't seen him around.'

Sam folded another bill, rustled it idly. Her eyes fastened on the money, fascinated.

Sam said: 'How well does Hugo Dare

know Muir? I'm trying to establish a link between them.'

'I don't know. Dare drops into the office sometimes. I wouldn't know what they talk about.'

Sam fed her the greenback to stimulate conversation.

'Last night,' he probed. 'Did Muir or Cabot leave the club? Was Dare here?'

Trixy shrugged.

'Muir was around most of the time. He might have gone out for a few minutes, difficult to say. I don't keep tabs on him. Cabot was in early in the evening, but I didn't see him later on. Why? What's this got to do with Irene? Did you find her at the Eucalyptus Drive address?'

Sam said: 'I found her.'

He didn't want to tell the blonde about the killing; she might shut up like a clam if she thought she were being involved in a murder case. He folded another dollar bill, pushed it into her hand.

'A bright girl like you can overhear things,' he said casually. 'If you get onto anything you think I ought to know, get in touch with me. I'll make it worth your while.'

He moved to the door, paused as a thought struck him.

'Did Muir ever mention the name, Wang Lee?'

Trixy shook her head.

'Never heard of him,' she said promptly.

Sam opened the door, looked out. The passage was empty. He stepped out, whispered:

'Give me a few minutes to get clear.'

She winked and tossed her head. She had a nice curve to her hips.

'Is that all you want?' she asked softly.

Sam grinned.

'Some other time, sugar. I'm busy right now.'

'Any time,' Trixy said. 'I told you, I've kinda taken a fancy to your mug!'

Sam went up the passage, passing Muir's office again. Voices mumbled inside but he couldn't pick out any words, and it was too dangerous to stop and listen at the keyhole. He went on, but not fast enough.

Hugo Dare and Paula blocked his path.

They had just come in from the club, arm in arm. Paula looked five hundred per cent. in something designed to prove she had It! Dare was smart in black evening dress with a white starched shirt and bow tie.

Dare's piercing black eyes stabbed into Sam's face. He raised his voice, called:

'Muir!'

The office door opened and Ambrose Muir, fair, slight, and blue-eyed looked out. He started as he saw Sam.

'Come into the office, Spain,' he said. 'We've things to talk over.'

Sam walked easily between Hugo Dare and the night club manager. He might be walking into trouble but he didn't let it bother him. He wanted to give Trixy the chance to get away.

Muir was too good a guesser though. He jerked open the dressing room door and looked in. His eyes were very cold as he saw Trixy.

'Get back on your job,' he grunted.

She went back to the club, scared, not looking at Sam. Paula laughed at her.

Muir said: 'So that's how you got the

Eucalyptus Drive address.'

'You're crazy,' Sam said evenly. 'I was fixing a hot date, that's all. Trixy's got the sort of shape I go for.'

They didn't look as if they believed him but Sam couldn't think of anything better.

'Into the office, Spain,' Muir repeated.

Sam stepped in, loosening his jacket so he could get at his Detective Special in a hurry. When he looked into the office, he didn't think he'd have the chance to use it.

Two men waited for him. One was Cabot, the slender man with the olive complexion. He had a gun in his hand, pointed at Sam's belly. His dark eye blazed with fury and his face was badly marked when someone had hit him.

Sam grinned, said:

'You should watch where you're walking, Cabot. Try walking through a brick wall next time!'

Sam turned to look at the second man. A large man with strong hands and an outsize in boots. He knew then who had beaten him up earlier that evening.

6

'I wouldn't try anything melodramatic, Spain,' Hugo Dare said warningly.

Sam Spain ignored him. He was looking over the large man and wondering if he could do anything about him if he ever got him alone.

He was a giant of a man perched on short, stumpy legs. His face was hairy and ugly with thick, protruding lips. His barrel-chest was covered by a sweat shirt and he wore tight-fitting slacks. The muscles of his long arms rippled like waves on a sea of flesh. A tough customer in anybody's language.

Cabot kept Sam covered. Paula immediately took Muir's chair. The way she flaunted herself around, Sam thought, was enough to get her into trouble. Muir closed the door and stood with his back to it. Hugo Dare took up a position facing Sam.

Sam lit a cigarette, placed it to his lips.

Cabot knocked it out, stamped his foot on it. He figured it would go over big if he acted tough.

'You've had one warning,' Dare said. 'Apparently it wasn't enough.'

Sam's grey eyes smiled bleakly and his lips tightened in a thin line. The large man said:

'Let me finish him, boss.'

Muir frowned.

'Quiet, Woodroffe — Dare's handling this, now.'

Sam wondered how three hundred pounds of muscle had ever got a name like Woodroffe. He didn't pursue the point very far because Hugo Dare was speaking again.

'I have no desire for further unpleasantness, Spain. Tell me where Irene Kline is and we'll say no more about your interference. The police are looking for her on a charge of murder — you don't want to become involved in that, do you?'

Sam didn't bother to reply. He figured he'd need all his breath when the action started. No-one had taken his gun away and he was hoping for a break.

Dare patted the artificial waves in his silver-grey hair. His tone was smooth and assured.

'I don't want trouble, Spain. Suppose I make a deal with you? I don't imagine you're making much money on this case — tell me where the redhead is and I'll pay you five thousand dollars, in cash.'

Sam laughed in his face.

'I'm a proud man, Hugo,' he said. 'I don't sell out my clients.'

Dare stepped back. His face turned white with anger and his lantern jaw seemed to grow even longer.

'That was stupid,' he said shortly. 'You'll have to be taught manners.'

'Let me take him,' Woodroffe grunted. 'I'll break him in pieces.'

Muir moved forward, smiling a little. He took Hugo Dare to one side, whispered something. Sam couldn't hear what they said; he contented himself with looking at Paula. Her crimson gown was strapless. Sam got ideas just looking at her. He'd never seen a woman before that had IT written all over her in capital letters.

She laughed softly, knowing what he was thinking. She crossed her legs carelessly, said:

'You can't afford me, Sam. I'm expensive — stick to your redhead. I'm strictly big-time.'

Sam said: 'You stick around with Hugo and you'll end up in the morgue. That's something new for you to think about. I hope it gives you something more to think about than where your next man's coming from.'

She came out of the chair, spitting. Her fingernails raked Sam's cheek, came away dripping blood.

'You dirty keyhole peeper!' she snarled. 'I'll claw your filthy eyes out!'

Dare pulled her back.

'Not now,' he said. 'Ambrose has a better idea.'

Sam tensed. What was coming? He measured the distance to the door, eyed Woodroffe in a calculating way. He was big, but he could be shifted. Cabot's gun dug into his back and he froze.

'Go on,' Cabot jeered, 'try it. I'd love to empty this magazine in your kidneys.'

Hugo Dare waved the gunman away. He smiled at Sam.

'We're letting you go this time, Spain, but keep your nose clean. Woodroffe, see him off the premises.'

Sam blinked. This was too smooth; there must be a catch in it somewhere. Woodroffe took his arm, pulled. Sam followed his arm through the door, along the passage to the rear exit of the 400 Club. Woodroffe kicked open the door and grabbed Sam round the waist. He lifted him in the air and threw him out. The door closed, blocking off the light.

Sam hit the ground with his shoulders, saving his face further damage. He rolled over, grabbing his Detective Special. He crouched in the shadows, waiting, but no attack came. It dawned on him that Dare was letting him get away. Why?

He couldn't work it out. He'd have to wait and see what happened — but whatever it was, Sam guessed he wasn't going to like it. Hugo Dare wouldn't play it that way.

Sam walked round to the Ford and drove off. He was tired and hungry.

Thinking could wait till tomorrow; right now, he wanted sleep. He travelled down Van Ness to Market Street, garaged his car and climbed the stairs to his apartment.

* * *

The telephone shrilled like a lost soul, cutting into Sam's sleep. He rolled off the bed, reaching out one hand for the receiver. The ringing stopped as he said, sleepily:

'Sam Spain. Who's ringing?'

'Oh, Sam.' It was Trixy's voice and she sounded agitated. 'I've got something for you and it can't wait. Come over to my place right away. 13 Ewing Terrace.'

'What — ' Sam started.

Hearing the click of the line going dead, he stopped. He replaced the receiver and lit a cigarette. The clock on the dressing table told him it was not quite eight in the morning.

Sam stripped off pyjamas, washed hurriedly in cold water. He dressed, strapping on a gun-holster and checking his Detective Special. He ran his fingers over the stubble on his chin; he needed a shave, but he didn't stop. Trixy sounded as if she wanted him there in a hurry. Maybe she'd got a line on Hugo Dare. Maybe the case was ready to break wide open.

He went down the stairs three at a time and got his Ford out of the garage. He smoked the cigarette as he drove; it was all the breakfast he was going to get that morning. He tried the whisky flask in the dashboard locker, cursed when he found it empty. A hell of a time to run out of liquor.

He put his foot on the accelerator as he went up Franklin Street, past the War Memorial, to swing left at Turk Street. He passed through Jefferson Square and kept on to Masonic Avenue. He turned right, then left into Ewing Terrace. The terrace was shaped like a horseshoe, went round in a circle to come out again on Masonic Avenue a block further north. There was no other way out and Sam didn't like that. He thought the set-up smelled like a trap.

Number thirteen was half-way round the horseshoe, a bungalow set in a microscopically small garden with a high wall at the back. The front door was half open. Sam went in, gun in hand. He called: 'Trixy!' And waited for the answer that never came.

The lines about Sam's mouth tightened till they looked as if they'd been etched in acid. He moved cat-footed down the passage, into the living room. A photograph and some items of feminine clothing told him that Trixy had lived there. He went down the passage to the bedroom.

The screaming of a police siren made him jump. He heard a patrol car brake outside and heavy footsteps sounded on the path to the front door. Sam went into the bedroom and suddenly understood what Ambrose Muir and Hugo Dare had been whispering about.

The blonde hung limply over the end of the bed, her face white, her hair trailing the carpet. Blood stained her diaphanous nightdress where she had been shot through the breast. Sam's Luger lay on the floor beside her. It was a neat frame-up.

Lieutenant Ernst came through the doorway with two uniformed cops. He said:

'Give me your gun, Sam.'

Sam looked at the tall Homicide man and scowled. He handed over his Detective Special. One of the cops looked at Trixy and whistled.

'Fancy knocking off a lush piece like that,' he growled.

Another car arrived in a hurry. Ambrose Muir came in, followed by Cabot. Muir looked shocked as he took in the scene.

'Poor Trixy,' he said. He stared at Sam and his voice grew cold. 'I see you've got the killer, lieutenant.'

Ernst snapped the brim of his hat and looked uncomfortable.

'I'm not so sure about that,' he said quietly.

Cabot had his gun out, covering Sam; he was hoping Sam would start something. Muir said:

'Spain did it all right. He threatened

Trixy, last night — I can bring forward half-a-dozen witnesses who heard him threaten her. He wanted to sleep with her and she turned him down.'

Sam spat: 'You filthy liar!'

Muir ignored him, speaking to the lieutenant.

'Trixy 'phoned me a little while back. She said Spain was trying to break in and asked me to protect her. That's why I rang you. Too bad we got here too late.'

Ernst inspected the Luger on the floor. He read off the number.

'Your gun, Sam?'

'Yeah, my gun. Two mugs beat me up, yesterday evening — they took the Luger away from me.'

Muir sneered: 'You'll have to think of something better than that.'

Sam spoke to Ernst.

'Cabot and another of Muir's men, a giant called Woodroffe, took the gun. Trixy sold me some information, that's why she's dead. Hugo Dare is behind this and the other killing, the Bartlett job. This is another frame.'

Ernst didn't say anything. Muir

scowled, smoothed his face into a smile.
He said:

'That is ridiculous. Cabot and Woodroffe have alibis. Spain's lying to save his
skin. He killed Trixy in a jealous rage,
because she wouldn't sleep with him. She
was alive a few minutes ago, because she
used the 'phone. Your doctor will confirm
she hasn't been dead long. Spain was in
the room — his gun fired the shot. What
more do you want?'

Ernst looked at Sam.

'You'd better come down to the station,
Sam. The D.A. will want to ask you a few
questions.'

Sam said: 'Okay.'

He moved for the door. He knew that if
the cops got him inside, he had no
chance. Dare would fake the evidence,
see that he didn't come out again. He'd
go to the electric chair. He couldn't let
Ernst take him . . .

Muir was off-guard. Sam caught his
arm, swung him into Cabot. Cabot's gun
went off — the slug hit the wall to the
right of Sam's head. Ernst made a grab at
Sam, but Sam beat him to the door. He

swung it shut in the lieutenant's face and ran down the passage.

He was through the front door before Ernst got after him again. Sam jumped into the Ford, raced the engine. He stepped on the accelerator as Cabot appeared on the porch. Cabot emptied his gun and the bullet-proof glass window on Sam's left shattered and scarred. But no slugs came through.

He drove wildly down Ewing Terrace, knowing that they'd be right after him. The terrace swung in a horseshoe curve and Sam was headed out — until another police car moved in ahead of him, blocking the road.

Sam was going too fast to stop. He swung the wheel, ran up the sidewalk. The Ford crashed a wooden fence, squeezed between the police car and a stone wall with a grating sound, and plunged on. At the corner, Sam turned left, right and left, onto Geary Street.

He braked the Ford, jumped out, ran for a street car going west. He travelled two blocks and jumped off. Opposite, a hotdog stand was doing good business with early-morning workers. Sam wedged himself into the crowd and got to the counter. He ordered coffee and a hotdog and leaned on the counter as if he had all the time in the world.

A police car flashed by, travelling fast. They wouldn't reckon on him going to ground so close to the bungalow; they'd expect him to run for it. Sam grinned and bit on the hotdog. He lit a cigarette and lingered over his coffee.

The crowd was dispersing around the stand. He'd be too conspicuous standing there any longer. He bad to get away before Ernst cordoned the area.

A wagon swung in to the curb to pick up a couple of labourers. Sam spoke to the driver.

'Which way you going, bud?'

'East to Leavenworth. Any use to yuh?'

Sam nodded and swung himself up onto the wagon.

'I'm late,' he said. 'I could use a lift that far.'

The wagon moved off, with Sam crouched on the metal floor, hidden by a dozen labourers. Another police car went by; no-one took any notice of a wagon-load of men going to work. Sam breathed easier.

He dropped off on the corner of Geary and Leavenworth and took a street car. He changed cars several times before he got within walking distance of the waterfront. Then he hoofed it to Joey's café and went in through the door in the yard. Joey was in the kitchen and he looked worried when he saw Sam. He said:

'Trouble, Sam. The girl's beat it!'

7

Sam Spain and Joey went up to the room at the top of the stairs. Sam drew the curtain and sat on the edge of the bed. He lit a cigarette and added the score. He didn't like the total — Hugo Dare was winning all along the line.

'Tell me about Irene,' he said.

Joey mopped his bald head and wrung fat hands.

'I'm sorry, Sam. I wouldn't have let this happen — '

Sam gestured with the glowing tip of his cigarette. It left a faint spiral of blue-grey smoke in the air. He said, quietly:

'I'm not blaming you, Joey. Just give me the facts.'

Joey's thick lips moved in speech.

'After you left, Sam, I told her to try and get some sleep. I left her alone up here because I had work to do in the café. I thought she would be okay after a rest, but — '

He took a deep breath and his bushy eyebrows went up and down.

'I took her some supper round about nine. She was sitting in the chair, staring into the mirror and talking to herself. It gave me the creeps to hear her. She wouldn't eat anything and didn't seem to know me. I guess her mind was giving way.'

Sam nodded, the lines about his mouth grim and harsh.

'Hugo gave her a rough time. She's never been treated like that before.'

Joey went on: 'She was muttering Dare's name over and over and saying he didn't love her, that no-one wanted her. It was embarrassing the way she went on talking and not taking any notice of me. I left her alone and went downstairs again.'

'Then she started pacing the room, up and down, up and down. It began to get on my nerves. And she never stopped talking. She was talking herself into a fury. When I went to bed, I gave her a couple of sleeping pills in a glass of water. I made her drink the stuff — enough to put a couple of elephants to sleep — but it had no effect on her. I guess she had things on her mind.'

Sam chain-lit a fresh cigarette, worrying over Irene.

'I went to bed,' Joey said, 'but didn't sleep much. I left the room of my door open so I could keep an eye on her. I'm telling you, Sam, I was worried about that girl. All night, she walked up and down, talking to herself, never stopping for a minute.'

'I dozed off and woke again. She was still at it, wearing a rut in the carpet and speaking Dare's name. I got up around six because I couldn't take it any more. I took her some breakfast and tried to get her to eat some. She left more than she ate.'

Joey mopped sweat off his forehead.

'By now, Irene was in a real lather. She hadn't a good word to say for Hugo Dare. She was talking about revenge, about making him pay for the rotten way he'd treated her. She said she was going to kill him!'

Sam's grey eyes grew bleak. His breath hissed sharply. Joey continued his story:

'I thought she'd wear herself out and drop off to sleep, so I went down to the café. Remember, she'd had no sleep and almost no food. I figured she'd keel over and wake up in a different frame of mind. She was on her way to the nut-house the way she was carrying on . . .

'So I left her alone. I was busy in the café and when I went upstairs again, she had gone. That was about eight o'clock. I panicked, thinking she'd wandered some-place where people would see her. I searched the house and the yard, then the waterfront, but I never found her. She was gone, all right, with no sign to say where.'

'Except she had Hugo Dare on her mind,' Sam pointed out.

Joey sweated some more.

'She wouldn't be crazy enough to go after Dare on her own!'

Sam drew on his cigarette, blew out a stream of smoke. He crushed out the butt and paced the room.

'You said yourself that she was heading for a breakdown, Joey. She wanted to kill Hugo . . . and she was in no fit state to weigh the odds. We can only hope the cops pick her up before she tangles with Dare's killers.'

Joey watched Sam pace the room. He said:

'Stop it! You remind me of *her* . . . '

Sam sat down again.

'What are you going to do now?' Joey asked. 'You going after her?'

'It isn't as easy as that,' Sam replied. He told Joey about Trixy, about the way Dare had framed him. Joey began to curse; he used a lot of obscene words to describe Hugo Dare.

After a silence, Joey suggested:

'Maybe Irene will come to her senses. She may come back here.'

Sam shook his head. The way Joey had described her he thought that unlikely.

'Hell hath no fury like a woman scorned,' he quoted. 'Whoever coined that phrase knew what he was talking about. I guess Hugo Dare won't bother anyone again if she does manage to reach him.'

Joey didn't say anything. Sam brooded.

'A private investigator is like a catalyst.

He speeds up the action, remaining unchanged at the end — if he's a good detective.'

'If he's alive at the end,' Joey remarked.

'That's what I mean!'

Sam paced the room again.

'Well, it's no good waiting. If the cops don't peg me, Dare will. If Irene's caught, she may talk about this place, then we'll have visitors. It's up to me to make the next move.'

'You'll want a gun,' Joey said. 'I've a .45 automatic I can let you have.'

He waddled away to his bedroom, returning with the gun and two boxes of shells. Sam loaded the automatic and shoved it home in his shoulder holster; he put the rest of the shells in his pocket.

'That's better,' he grunted. 'I feel half-naked without a gun. Now I'm ready to talk turkey with Dare and his killers. I'll want a car, too. Can you fix that, Joey.'

The fat man nodded.

'I'll hire one from the garage round the corner.'

'Do that,' he said, 'and bring me notepaper and a pen. I want to write a letter while you're gone.'

Sam sat at the table and began to write. He addressed the envelope to Lieutenant Ernst, at his home address. Sam wanted to make sure that Ernst got it; the lieutenant was an honest cop and he'd follow up the leads Sam gave him.

Sam wrote a full report, detailing what had happened from the time Mrs. Kline walked into his office. He told of his visit to the 400 Club and how Trixy had given him the Eucalyptus Drive address. He described how he'd gone to the bungalow and found Bartlett's corpse, his consequent talk with Irene and their call at Hugo Dare's west side residence. He told how he'd hidden the girl without saying where — not wishing to involve Joey.

He omitted to describe he'd altered Irene's appearance and that she'd disappeared. He mentioned his visit to Commercial Street, the fact that Bartlett had been a heroin addict, how he'd been beaten up by Cabot and Woodroffe and his Lugar stolen. He gave Wang Lee's address in Pagoda Place and told how the Chinese had refused to talk.

110

He mentioned his second visit to the 400 Club and how Hugo Dare had offered him five thousand dollars to surrender Irene. He described Muir's plan to frame him for the killing of Trixy.

Joey came back as Sam sealed the envelope.

'Car's outside,' the fat man said. 'You want me to come with you?'

Sam shook his head.

'You'll be more use here, Joey. I may run into Irene and bring her back. And I may want to hide out here myself. So you stay out of it — the less the cops know about you the better. That way, I'll always have one hide-out I can rely on.'

'Okay, Sam, whatever you say. I guess you know I'd carry a gun for you any time — you've only to ask.'

Sam clapped him on the shoulder. His grey eyes smiled.

'Thanks, Joey, I'll remember. You can do one thing for me — see that this letter is posted as soon as possible. Use a Market Street mailbox so as not to give them a lead.'

Joey slipped the letter in his pocket.

'I'll do that.'

Sam went down to the yard and viewed the car. It was a green Humber, a six-cylinder job with plenty of power. Sam grinned; Joey had the idea Sam might want to go places in a hurry. Well, he might be right, at that.

Sam got behind the wheel and headed up Third Street. He drove carefully, watching traffic lights. He didn't want a cop to peg him for some minor offence right now. He wanted to get to the 400 Club and pick up either Muir or Cabot. He wanted to get one of them alone and work him over — Sam was prepared to get tough if they wouldn't talk.

Thoughts of Irene bothered him. Where was she? What was she aiming to do? If she went to Dare's house openly, she'd run into a load of trouble. Whatever happened, someone was going to be hurt.

The Humber crossed Market Street and went up Kearny to Columbus Avenue, passing through North Beach. Sam travelled west along Bay Street to pick up Marina Boulevard. He parked the car and watched the entrance to the 400 Club.

He sat in the car, smoking and waiting. Someone would have to show up, sooner or later, then he would go into action. It was quiet on the Boulevard. The bay sparkled beyond the park behind him; a few cars moved in the direction of the Golden Gate Bridge.

Half-an-hour passed, then Cabot came out of the club. Sam tensed; this was it. The olive-skinned gunman was alone and he didn't take any notice of the Humber parked across the way. Sam watched him start a Studebaker and drive west. The green Humber moved after him.

Cabot wasn't in a hurry; he drove easily, taking his time at intersections. Sam let him get ahead; he didn't want the gunman to suspect he was being trailed. He just kept the Studebaker in sight, thinking of all the things he could do to Cabot to make him talk. Sam didn't enjoy thoughts of that kind but it was the only sort of persuasion Cabot would understand and, with a murder rap hanging over him, Sam couldn't afford to be fussy.

Cabot travelled down Divisadero Street with Sam a block behind him. There was plenty of other traffic about so he didn't take any notice of the Humber. He kept going, down Castro Street to 31st. He swung right along Diamond, turned into Berkeley Street.

Sam let him go. He knew that Berkeley was a dead end; Cabot couldn't go further, couldn't turn back without running into him. That was how Sam liked it.

Sam parked the Humber and proceeded on foot. The houses were spaced far apart; that was good too. He saw the Studebaker outside the house at the end of the street, and smiled.

The set-up was perfect. Cabot was inside the end house, well out of calling distance of his neighbours; Sam didn't think they'd be interrupted. He hefted the .45 automatic in his hand as he went up the path.

Sam tried the front door; it wouldn't open. He moved quietly to a side window that was open and climbed through.

Cabot was in the bedroom packing a suitcase.

Sam said: 'Don't bother — you're not going any place, Cabot.'

The gunman spun round grabbing for his revolver. He stopped, stood quite still when he saw the heavy automatic in Sam's hand.

'That's right,' Sam said. 'Don't force me to use this — .45 slugs make quite a hole. And I'll shoot you in the belly, where it hurts most. You'll be a long time dying, Cabot.'

Cabot began to sweat. His padded shoulders sagged; his greasy, olive face glistened under tiny beads of sweat.

He said: 'What do you want, Spain?'

Sam relieved him of his gun.

'Over against the bed,' he ordered. 'Turn around.'

Cabot obeyed. Sam slugged him with the .45 and pushed him so he went on the bed as he fell. He rolled him over, tore the sheets into strips and tied him down. He gagged him, then went through the house. It was unlikely Cabot had company but Sam was taking no chances.

He found no-one.

Sam returned to the bedroom to throw a jug of cold water over Cabot. The slim man moved and opened dark eyes. Sam took off his gag. Cabot said:

'You won't get away with this.'

Sam laughed unpleasantly.

'Maybe you'll change your mind.'

He hit Cabot in the face with the barrel of his automatic. Cabot winced as the gunsight opened his cheek. Blood ran into the corners of his mouth and he licked the salty stuff. Sam hit him again, across the mouth, breaking his front teeth. Cabot choked and tears ran down his face.

'That's just to prove I'm not kidding,' Sam said grimly. 'Now we'll have a little talk. Tell me what I want to know and maybe I won't hurt you. Maybe. Hold out on me and you'll pray for a quick death — and you won't get it.'

Cabot snarled: 'You can't make me talk!'

Sam hit him again, on the nose. Cabot wanted to scream but Sam forced the gag into his mouth, choking off his cries.

'The way I figure it,' Sam said calmly, 'is that you bumped Bartlett at Muir's order. You killed Trixy, too — that's how you got to the bungalow so quickly. You want to make a statement?'

Cabot said: 'Go to hell!'

Sam hit him to hurt this time. The heavy automatic slammed across Cabot's face, breaking the bridge of his nose with a sound like steel wire snapping. Cabot blubbered. Sam forced the gun into his mouth. He said:

'You got the idea I'm not playing charades? You're going to talk — or die. And don't think I won't kill you. I'd as soon work over Muir to get what I want. It won't lose me any sleep if I blow your head off.'

Cabot made moaning noises. Sam took the gun out of his mouth and Cabot croaked.

'For God's sake, Spain — don't hit me any more. I can't take it any more . . .'

His greasy face was running with sweat and tears mixed up with his blood. Sam said:

'Tell me about Bartlett — and Trixy.'

Cabot gagged on a broken tooth. Sam threw more water in his face and placed the muzzle of the .45 to one of the gunman's eyes.

'Talk!'

'All right, I'll talk,' Cabot whined. 'Muir told me to kill Bartlett. The idea was to frame the Kline girl — '

'How'd you get Bartlett to the bungalow?' Sam questioned.

'Paula invited him. I guess he thought he was on a hot date when he went there.'

'Yeah,' Sam said, 'and he got an ice-pick instead. Go on!'

'Muir wanted to get you out of the way — you were making trouble by investigating Bartlett's death. That's why Trixy was bumped — and to stop her talking any more.'

'You shot her?'

'Yes. Muir told me to — '

'Where does Hugo Dare figure in this? Why did Bartlett have to die?'

'I don't know,' Cabot mumbled. 'Dare gives the orders and Muir passes them on to us. I don't know why Bartlett had to be bumped — '

Sam's finger tightened round the trigger.

'All right, Cabot, start praying — this is it!'

'No — no! I swear I'm telling the truth. I don't know why Hugo wanted Bartlett knocked off — he had the girl framed to clear himself. That's all I know — I swear it!'

Sweat poured down his face as he stared into the ugly muzzle of Sam's .45. Sam put the gag back in Cabot's mouth and sat down at the table. He wrote out what the gunman had told him.

'Listen, Cabot. This is your confession. You're going to sign it, then I'll put pressure on Muir. That way I'll get to the top man, Hugo Dare. Maybe I'll spoil Paula's sex-appeal on the way . . . but if you don't sign this, you won't know anything about that!'

He untied Cabot's right hand and put the pen in his hand. He put the paper on a book under his hand and shoved his gun into Cabot's face.

'Sign!'

Cabot signed. Sam waved the paper till

it dried. He was feeling good. Muir and Hugo Dare would have to think fast to get out of that one. Things were looking up. He tied Cabot's arm again.

Sam put away his gun, buttoned his coat. He shoved Cabot's confession in his pocket, said:

'I think I'll have a talk with Ambrose.'

A smooth voice said:

'I'd like that, Spain.'

Sam turned slowly to face the gun in Muir's hand. Behind the night club manager, Woodroffe loomed like something from a nightmare. Muir's blue eyes were very cold and his trigger-finger dangerously taut. Sam didn't move.

'Take his gun, Woodroffe — and the paper.'

The giant came up behind Sam, keeping out of line of Muir's gun. Sam felt familiar large hands grip him in a vice; one hand took his .45, Cabot's confession.

Woodroffe kept Sam covered with his own gun while Muir read the confession. No-one took any notice of the man on the bed.

120

'That was smart thinking, Spain,' Muir said softly. 'It might have worked if I hadn't been expecting Cabot back in a hurry. That was something you overlooked. When he didn't show up, I got worried, so I came to see what was wrong.'

He waved the paper, and smiled.

'It was a good thing I did!'

Sam watched Ambrose Muir bring a silver-plated cigarette lighter from his pocket. He flicked the wheel, held the paper over the flame. Sam felt suddenly weak as he saw Cabot's confession burn before his eyes. Muir ground the ashes under foot.

He said: 'That won't do you any good, Spain.'

The man on the bed made wriggling movements; he wanted to be set free. Ambrose Muir went across and stood over Cabot, looking down at him, his blue eyes cold as ice. Woodroffe dug the muzzle of the .45 into Sam's back to discourage any ideas he might have.

'You shouldn't have talked, Cabot,' Muir said softly. 'You shouldn't have signed that confession. It means I can't trust you any more.'

He brought his revolver to bear on Cabot's heart, wrapped the barrel in the bedclothes to muffle the sound. He squeezed the trigger once — once was enough. Cabot jerked as the slug tore into his heart; his head dropped back at a strange angle and he went slack. He died without a sound.

Muir looked at Sam.

'The police want you for Trixy's murder,' he said. 'If I were to shoot you in self-defence, no-one would bother . . . on the other hand, I want the girl. Irene Kline. Dare doesn't like it because she hasn't been caught yet. Perhaps I can persuade you to tell me where she is.'

'Like hell you can!' Sam said.

Muir smiled coldly.

'Put him to sleep, Woodroffe.'

Sam tried to dodge the heavy automatic. He was too late. It slammed down on his skull and he blacked out.

8

Joey was busy in the kitchen when Irene Kline walked out, through the yard to the waterfront. The docks were beginning to come alive for the day's work as she turned into Army Street.

The morning air was chilly and she shivered a little as the wind cut through her thin blouse; she had no coat, no money, only the clothes Sam had bought her and a burning desire for revenge. The down-at-heel shoes didn't fit properly and by the time she reached Mission Street, she had blisters on both heels.

She walked down Mission Street as if in a trance. Her legs moved automatically, carrying her across Alemany Boulevard and Silver Avenue. There were dark rings under her eyes from lack of sleep; her stomach was empty but she didn't feel hunger.

She moved along the sidewalks, quickly, not seeing people, crossing roads in a way that made car drivers use their brakes in a hurry. Irene was hardly aware of the world around her; she thought only of Hugo Dare and what she was going to do to him.

Her head throbbed like a drum beating out a savage rhythm — revenge. How she hated the man who had scorned her! He would die . . . she would kill him, then the beating in her head would stop, the emptiness of her heart be filled.

She muttered to herself as she went along, repeating Hugo's name. A man looked at her, said:

'You all right, miss ? You look ill. If there's anything I can do . . .'

Irene didn't stop. She hurried by without speaking. They wanted to stop her killing Hugo; they all wanted to stop her reaching the house on west side. But she wasn't going to let them.

She had been walking for over an hour now and her legs began to ache. She slowed down, turning into Ocean Avenue. She would have collapsed if it hadn't been for the terrible thoughts churning through her head . . . vengeance!

At Balboa Park, she picked up San Jose

Avenue and headed south-west. The sun was higher now, bathing her in its warm rays. Dust covered her shoes and she wore a hole in the heel of one stocking. She went along Lobos Street to Randolph, kept going till she made Lake Merced Boulevard.

Irene plodded round the edge of the lake, tired and determined. Nothing could stop her now. She struck due west, across the sand dunes. She could see Dare's house and that brought new energy to her lagging feet.

She struggled across the dunes to the house. Sand filled her shoes. She began to run, her eyes burning with the feverish desire to kill. Her breath came in sharp gasps; her whole body was rigid, tensed; her hands clenched so that the knuckles turned white.

She reached the wall bordering the grounds and tried to climb it. The wall was too high; she had to move back, take a run and spring at it. Her fingers curled round the top of the wall and she pulled herself up. There was glass set in jagged edges along the wall-top; the glass cut her fingers and blood ran down her arms. She tore her skirt getting over.

Irene dropped into the grounds of Dare's house. She moved between the trees, across the lawn, past flowering shrubs and silent statuettes. She reached the back part of the house and entered through a rear door.

Inside the house, it was quiet. She saw the butler and waited, seething with impatience, while he went away. She wasn't going to let the butler stop her reaching Hugo; she remembered he'd tried once before. She found the tiled hall and climbed the stairway curving upwards to another floor. She went up the stairs and along the passage to double oak doors.

Irene didn't pause. She had no weapon, no idea how she was going to kill Hugo Dare. But her craving for revenge was too strong for caution; she pushed open the doors and went in.

'Hugo — '

She stopped suddenly, stood motionless as she saw that the man she sought was not in the room. Paula was alone on the divan.

The blonde swung round, her eyes widening as she saw Irene in the doorway. She said:

'How did *you* get here?'

Irene came into the room, moving towards the blonde.

'Where's Hugo — I'm going to kill him!'

Her voice was so flat, so emotionless, that Paula came off the divan in a hurry. She was scared. She looked at Irene, at her ragged, dyed hair, her soiled blouse and torn skirt. Blood dripped from Irene's fingers and her eyes burned with a terrible light.

Paula saw it was no time for wise-cracks. She said:

'Hugo's out. I don't know when he'll be back.'

That stopped Irene cold. She hadn't thought exactly how she'd kill Dare, only that she would — somehow. His absence upset her plans; she didn't know what to do.

She stood there, looking at Paula and trying to make up her mind. She felt suddenly tired. She wanted to sit down, to rest. She wouldn't sleep — she'd just sit down and wait for Hugo. It had been a long walk, across San Francisco. She'd kill Hugo when he returned.

She moved towards the divan and sat down. Paula stepped back hurriedly. To her, Irene was a mad woman with a lust to kill. She didn't want to be the victim of a homicidal maniac.

Irene watched Paula. The blonde was beautiful in a sensual way and she was wearing something sheer and semi-transparent which enhanced her sex-appeal. Irene thought about the blonde and began to remember.

'You took Hugo away from me,' she said. 'You laughed — '

Paula knew she had to stop Irene thinking that way, before she got around to transfering her hatred from Hugo to herself. She backed to the wall, not taking her eyes off Irene.

'You look all in,' she said. 'You need a drink.'

Paula's hand shook as she poured a large whisky. She handed it to Irene.

'It'll make you feel better,' she encouraged.

Irene realized how thirsty she was; it had been a long walk and her throat was parched. She sipped the whisky. It warmed her — she drank deeply.

'Hugo,' she murmured, 'I must kill Hugo . . .'

She sank back on the cushions. The whisky made her sleepy. She hadn't had anything to eat for a long time and the alcohol did funny things to her empty stomach. Her eyes closed . . .

Paula saw her chance. She poured another whisky, pushed it into Irene's hand.

'Drink this,' she whispered urgently.

Irene didn't want it, but she was too tired to fight against the way Paula forced the glass to her lips. The fiery liquid burned as it slipped down her throat. Her limbs were heavy; her head nodded sleepily.

'Kill Hugo . . .'

Paula laughed softly. She'd turned the tables. Dare would be pleased to have the girl handed over to him. She seized a gun to cover Irene, in case she woke, then picked up the telephone.

★ ★ ★

Sam Spain's eyes blinked open. His head throbbed and his body was cramped. He tried to move his arms and discovered that he couldn't. He was strapped down, helpless.

Woodroffe's ugly face loomed over him.

'You're awake, huh?' the giant said. 'The boss will be pleased.'

Sam glared at Woodroffe. He licked his lips, said:

'Thanks for the lump on the head — one day I'll repay it with interest.'

Woodroffe guffawed loudly.

'I could take you with one hand tied!'

He crossed the room and went out through a door behind hanging curtains. Sam twisted his head to survey the room. They'd moved him from the house in Berkeley Street.

He was in a room without windows. The oriental drapes and smell of incense told him he was back in Wang Lee's House of the Seven Moons in China-town. He was lying on a table, bound with thick leather straps, and he had been stripped to the waist. Sam didn't like that idea; he liked it even less when he saw the coke brazier in the corner and the selection of irons heating in it. He wrestled with the straps, without loosening them.

Wang Lee came in, followed by Hugo Dare and Woodroffe.

'The terror of Lawbreakers has returned to the humble home of Wang Lee,' the Chinese mocked. 'My prayers have been answered.'

Woodroffe sat on a chair by the door, a gun in his hand. Dare moved across to look down into Sam's face. His lantern jaw champed on a cigar and his piercing black eyes were alight with sadistic pleasure. His distinguished air left him; the brutal nature of the gangster lay revealed.

'You're going to talk, Spain; get that idea firmly fixed in your head. You're going to tell me where you've hidden Irene Kline. Wang Lee is expert at the task of opening stubborn mouths . . . you can save yourself a lot of pain by speaking now.'

Sam didn't reply. He had no idea where Irene was — and Dare wouldn't believe that. Too, he had no intention of giving Joey away.

Wang Lee stroked his long, waxed moustache. His face was an evil mask as he gloated over his victim.

'It will give me the greatest pleasure if you prolong the torture till you can stand it no longer, Master of Spies. A man who speaks before he must is a coward — and he deprives me of the intense satisfaction of forcing his tongue to wag. You may scream without fear of being over-heard . . .'

He crossed to the brazier and selected a red-hot needle with a pair of tongs. Sam watched him bring the needle closer; the tip pricked his bare chest — sank in, searing the flesh. Sam's lips tightened in pain. He could smell his skin burning, feel the red-hot needle slide into his chest. Sweat broke out on his forehead and he wondered how much of Wang Lee's devilish torture he could stand.

Wang Lee left the needle sticking in Sam's chest and went back to the brazier.

With the tongs, he pulled another red-hot sliver of steel from the coals. He never hurried as he moved back to the table. Sam watched the needle come lower. Wang Lee drew the glowing tip across Sam's bare flesh, leaving a burning, searing scar. The needle seemed to sink in of its own accord; the Chinese put no pressure on it. Sam quivered with agony; his lips parted and he had to bite his tongue to stop himself crying out.

'The art of torture is one best learnt by patience,' Wang Lee murmured. 'The essence of pain-giving is slowness; the victim must be given time to anticipate the agony to come. It must be inflicted with finesse . . . '

He left the second needle in Sam's flesh and returned to the brazier. Dare leant over Sam, smiling cruelly. He said:

'Ready to talk, Spain. Wang Lee can go on for hours, if need be. Where's the girl?'

The Chinese returned with a fresh needle. Sam winced as the steel tip scorched the hair on his chest; the acrid smell of burning hair and skin made him shudder. Then came the sharp, searing agony of the needle going into his flesh. He writhed under the straps, his lungs gasping for air. Wang Lee withdrew his tongs, leaving a third needle projecting from Sam's chest.

'This is the merest preliminary,' he explained. 'I want to test your resistance to pain. Later, I shall operate on the more tender parts of your body, the muscles, the stomach. One man I played with took thirty-two needles in the stomach without fainting . . . do you think you will beat his powers of endurance, Prince of Detectives?'

Sam swore.

'I'll kill you, Wang Lee — I'll swear I'll kill you, you devil!'

The Chinese smiled complacently. He brought another steel needle from the glowing coals, buried it in Sam's chest muscles.

'Later,' he promised, 'I shall concentrate on the face. It is the eyes that usually persuade a man to talk. Of course, one must be careful not to let the needle penetrate the brain — half-an-inch is enough. Enough to sear the jelly of the eyeball. I can assure you the pain is intense . . . '

Dare said: 'Where's the girl, Spain?'

Sam spat in his face.

'You're wasting your time, Hugo. I don't know where she is — she walked out on me and I haven't seen her since.'

Wang Lee used a fifth needle, smiling evilly.

'I am glad you are stubborn, King of Investigators. I shall enjoy your screams when the pain becomes unendurable . . . and, later, you will tell us where the girl is hidden. It is a question of time!'

The sixth needle plunged into Sam's bared flesh. The muscles of his chest contracted with the burning agony; the smell of scorched skin grew worse. Sam struggled against the leather straps; anger surged through him. He wanted to get free, to get his hands on Wang Lee and Hugo Dare. He swore he'd have no mercy on them if he ever got his hands free.

His head began to reel as the Chinese continued to push red-hot needles into his flesh. He felt faint; his head went lax, his eyes closed and consciousness began to fade.

Dare said: 'He's passing out. Get some water, Woodroffe.'

Icy cold water slashed Sam's face and chest. He revived.

Dare said: 'Tell me where Irene Kline is and this will stop.'

Sam gasped as Wang Lee pulled out the now cold needles from his chest with a pair of pincers. Charred flesh came away with the steel slivers and blood started to run over Sam's ribs.

He said: 'I don't know where the girl is — and that's the truth. You're wasting your time, Hugo.'

Wang Lee used bellows to liven the brazier. He shoved the needles deep into the glowing coals.

'The All-seeing Eye will change his opinion soon. I shall use his face for a pin-cushion as soon as the needles are red-hot!'

Woodroffe looked down at Sam as if wondering how any man could stand such punishment.

'Maybe he's telling the truth,' he

grunted. 'Maybe he really doesn't know where the redhead is. I guess he'd talk if he did — no man would take those needles if he could stop it by talking.'

Dare sneered: 'You don't know Spain. He fancies himself as a knight in shining armour, protecting the girl from harm. Wang Lee will soon change his mind. Spain knows where Irene Kline is, all right.'

Wang Lee drew a needle from the fire with his tongs and moved towards Sam. The tip was cherry red. Sam tried to draw back, but he was helpless. He felt the needle tip touch his face, then the steel sank into his cheek. He couldn't stop the moaning sound that came out of his mouth; the pain was too much.

Dare chuckled.

'He's breaking, Wang Lee. Work on one of his eyes. We haven't got a week to make him talk — the longer that girl is at large, the longer my neck's in danger. I want her caught, sentenced, and sent to the chair.'

Wang Lee left the needle sticking out from Sam's cheek. He went back to the brazier.

'The right eye,' he murmured. 'The Emperor of Finders-out shall lose the sight of his right eye in a long moment of searing pain. He will scream in excruciating agony . . .'

Sam sweated. He gritted his teeth, struggled desperately to break the straps holding him. They held. A cold fear seized him as he watched the Chinese walk slowly towards him, carrying another red-hot needle. He shuddered as he imagined the hot steel sinking into his eyeball. He closed his eyes tightly and bit his tongue to stop himself giving Wang Lee the pleasure of hearing him scream.

Wang Lee forced his right eye open. Tears flooded up in Sam's eye as he watched the glowing red tip of the needle come closer. He writhed in mental agony, but could do nothing to save himself.

The needle moved towards his eyeball, slowly, slowly . . . and the telephone shrilled loudly.

Dare picked up the 'phone, spoke into it. Wang Lee withdrew the needle from within a half-inch of Sam's eyeball and chuckled.

'Your screaming must not be heard over the telephone,' he smirked. 'I shall heat the needle again, Prince of Detectives; you may have a few more minutes contemplation of the agony to come — that will increase my pleasure and it may persuade you to divulge the hiding place of Irene Kline.'

Hugo Dare put down the telephone. He was grinning happily.

'That won't be necessary, Wang Lee. Paula has the girl a prisoner at my house!'

'A pity,' Wang Lee sighed. 'It would have given me so much satisfaction to burn out the eyes of the King of Investigators.'

'No time for playing around,' Hugo Dare snapped. 'You start shifting the stuff to the 400 Club. I'm going back to deal with the girl. Woodroffe, finish Spain and dump his body in the bay!'

9

Someone was slapping her face. Irene
Kline came awake suddenly. Her head
spun and her stomach somersaulted. Her
breath smelled of alcohol.

'Wake up, you slut!'

Paula's voice grated in her ears. It was
the blonde who was slapping her. Irene
sat up and began to take notice. The first
thing she noticed was Hugo Dare's
smiling face.

She got up, starting to move towards
him. Automatically, she said:

'I'm going to kill you, Hugo.'

Paula knocked her back on the divan.
Dare produced a gun and pointed it in
her face. He laughed.

'It was nice of you to call, Irene. The
cops are on their way to arrest you for
murder — and if you try to get away, I'll
shoot you down.'

Irene began to remember things. Paula
had made her drink too much whisky and

she'd gone to sleep; now it was too late to get at Hugo . . . or was it. She came off the divan like a tigress deprived of its young. Her fingers raked Hugo's face; she wanted to claw out his eyes — to get her hands about his throat.

Dare hit her with the barrel of his gun. She fell backwards on the divan, holding her face. Her hands came away, covered in blood.

'You swine,' she sobbed. 'I'll tell them what really happened — I'll — '

Dare hit her again.

'Shut up!' he snarled. 'No-one is going to take any notice of what you say. You'll burn for the murder of Clint Bartlett.'

Paula laughed.

'I hope she spins that yarn about you being a secret service agent — that'll sure cook her goose. No jury will believe her.'

Irene said: 'You won't get away with this. Sam will get you — '

Hugo Dare smiled pleasantly.

'Spain is dead,' he replied. 'His body will be fished out of the bay. Your only hope has gone.'

Irene started to cry. Sam dead! It was

only then that she realized she had fallen in love with Sam. She hated Hugo more than ever. She tried to get at him again.

Dare stepped back, cursing. He swung his fist, hit her hard in the face. Irene gave a strangled cry and slumped sideways, holding her face and moaning piteously. She fell in a heap on the carpet.

'You bitch!' Paula snapped. 'Shut that bloody row!'

The blonde kicked Irene in the face with her pointed shoes. Hugo Dare grinned at Paula. He lit a cigar, said:

'You dames sure love each other!'

Paula stopped kicking Irene. She moved towards Dare, swaying voluptuously. She pressed her sensuous body to Dare's, lifting her lips.

'I've got to have some fun, Hugo — you've been away all morning.'

He pushed her off.

'Later, Paula. I want to get this matter cleared up first. The police — '

He stopped as the door opened and the butler announced:

'Lieutenant Ernst.'

Irene crawled along the floor, pulled

herself onto the divan. She looked at the tall, lanky man who came in. There was something about his swarthy face, his tiny bright eyes, that appealed to her. He snapped the brim of his hat at Dare, looked at Irene, and said quietly:

'Was that necessary, Dare? I don't hold with beating up women.'

Hugo Dare puffed on his cigar, smiling broadly.

'She's a killer, lieutenant. She murdered Bartlett, then tried to finish me. I had to get rough to protect myself — and Paula. But she's all yours now; take her away and set the wheels of justice in motion.'

Ernst sat down and lit a cigarette. He seemed to be in no hurry.

'There's one or two points to this case that bear investigation,' he said. 'I'd like to hear the girl's story before I take her in. Suppose we talk it over?'

Dare didn't like that. He snapped.

'You're exceeding your authority, lieutenant. Your job is to follow orders. The D.A. wants Irene Kline for murder — you arrest her and leave the thinking to him.'

Ernst leaned forward.

'That's what I mean,' he said. 'Someone's putting pressure on the D.A. Someone wants Miss Kline out of the way before she has the chance to open her mouth. Why?'

Dare shrugged.

'I don't know what you're talking about.'

Paula snapped:

'Watch yourself, lieutenant. You may find yourself pounding a beat again if you start acting without orders.'

Ernst looked at the blonde. His eyes showed no admiration for her sensuous beauty, scarcely concealed by the gauzy negligee she wore with careless ease.

'You ought to put some clothes on,' he said pointedly.

Paula flushed. Ernst ignored her, turned to Irene.

'Let's hear your side of it,' he suggested.

Dare protested: 'Really, this isn't necessary — '

Ernst drew his revolver and squinted along the barrel. He waved it casually. His voice was very quiet.

'I think it would be a good idea to hear Miss Kline.'

Dare swallowed hard; he said nothing. Paula moved towards the lieutenant, smiling at him.

'I'm sure,' she murmured huskily, 'that we can find something more interesting to talk about, lieutenant — after you've taken the girl to the station.'

Ernst didn't smile. His voice went flat.

'I've seen better approaches on Market Street, sister. Why don't you go back where you belong?'

Paula went white with rage.

'You lousy copper,' she snarled. 'You filthy keyhole peeper — '

Dare shut her up. Ernst touched Irene's arm.

'Tell it,' he said.

Irene told it. She told how Hugo had sworn he'd loved her, had promised to marry her. She mentioned the secret service story Hugo had spun her; she told him she'd never seen Bartlett, that Hugo had laughed when she'd gone to him, with Sam. She talked about the way Sam had promised to help her break the frame-up. She didn't, of course, know about Trixy's death and the fact that Sam, too, was wanted for murder . . .

'Where's Sam now?' Ernst questioned.

Irene wiped tears from her eyes. She looked accusingly at Hugo Dare.

'He's killed Sam,' she said bitterly. 'He said Sam's body has been thrown in the bay.'

Ernst went rigid. He turned his gun towards Dare.

'If that's true,' he said flatly, 'I'll get you mister. Sam was a buddy of mine.'

Dare puffed on his cigar, smiling.

'It's fantastic,' he protested. 'If Spain *is* dead, why, she must have killed him!'

Ernst said: 'I've known Sam a long time. He was an honest cop. If he backed up Miss Kline's story, it was because he believed her. That leaves you wide open, Dare.'

'Spain may have been misled,' Hugo Dare said smoothly. 'Bartlett and the girl were lovers. She lived in the bungalow he paid for — she killed him . . . '

'Maybe,' Ernst said, rising to his feet.

'I'm taking the girl in for questioning — and she's going to get a chance to tell her side of it. If Sam hadn't skipped with her, the case would have been sewn up by now. But things have happened since then. Trixy got bumped — and I don't figure Sam Spain as the sort of guy to go around knocking off girls because they refuse to sleep with him. I know Sam better than that.'

He slipped his gun back in its holster and tapped Irene on the shoulder.

'You come with me, Miss Kline. Someone framed Sam — so maybe you're telling the truth. I'm going to find out.'

Dare said: 'You're running into trouble, lieutenant.'

Ernst snapped the brim of his hat.

'It happens in my job,' he said quietly.

Irene wiped her face and stood up. She smiled at Ernst.

'You're a friend of Sam's,' she said. 'I'll do what you say.'

The door opened quietly and Ambrose Muir came through, a gun in his hand.

'This looks like being quite a party,' he said. 'No — don't move lieutenant!'

Ernst stood still. He said:

'It's always a mistake to shoot a cop. Even crooked politicians can't get away with that.'

Dare took Ernst's gun away from him.

'I figure we can,' he purred. 'You know too much to be allowed to go free.'

He rang the bell and told the butler to fetch a rope. The butler was quick. Ernst sat in a chair, at gun-point, while the butler tied him down. Paula took care of Irene; the blonde seemed to have taken a dislike to her.

'What's the set-up?' Muir asked.

Dare was all smiles now. He was enjoying the situation as much as his cigar. He smoothed out the artificial waves in his silver-grey hair.

'This is the way we'll work it. The girl knocked off Bartlett, Sam Spain and the lieutenant — we'll take care of him presently, away from the house. Spain killed Trixy. That accounts for everything — and we'll get a confession out of the girl to clinch matters. Then she can go to the chair.'

'I won't sign any confession,' Irene

sobbed. 'I won't!'

Only Paula took any notice of her. The blonde hit her again.

'There's Cabot,' Muir said.

Dare considered the point.

'That's true. All right, Spain bumped Cabot.' He grinned. 'We'll say that Cabot died defending Trixy's honour!'

Paula jeered: 'That's a laugh!'

Muir's blue eyes held a puzzled expression.

'There's something else. Irene Kline went to ground somewhere, with a friend of Spain's. We ought to attend to that point.'

Hugo Dare nodded. He stroked his lantern jaw.

'She'll tell us where she hid out,' he said, looking at Irene. 'We'll send a couple of boys with a tommy-gun to seal up that end of it. The whole thing's watertight.'

'I won't tell you anything,' Irene said.

She tried to get at Hugo again. Paula blocked her off.

'I'll make her talk,' Dare said confidently. 'Wang Lee isn't the only one with ideas in that line.'

He left the room, returning shortly with another rope and a glass bottle. He carried the bottle carefully, so as not to spill any of the liquid on himself. Irene struggled, but she didn't have a chance. She was tied to a chair, helpless.

Dare removed the stopper from the bottle. The liquid was colourless and gave off pungent fumes. He shoved the bottle under Irene's nose and she jerked her head back, tears running down her face.

'Nitric acid,' Dare said. 'She'll talk!'

He set the bottle down on a table, scribbled some lines on a notepad. He read aloud what he had written.

'I killed Clint Bartlett because we quarrelled over money. I killed Sam Spain because he found out about me. I killed Lieutenant Ernst for the same reason.'

Ernst said: 'Even you can't get away with this, Dare. Not everyone at City Hall is as crooked as you. Someone will smell a rat.'

Muir prodded him with his gun.

'Shut up. You're not in this.'

Irene's arm was freed from the elbow. Dare gave her a pen, said:

'Sign it!'

She threw the pen down, sobbing.

'I won't! I won't!'

Dare smiled. He was in no hurry. The girl would sign, he was sure of that. Nothing could go wrong now; Spain was dead and there was no-one else he feared. There could be no interruptions. He would play with the girl till she signed the paper.

'Spain gave me the idea of a written confession,' he said. 'He tried it on Cabot. But even Spain didn't think of using acid.'

He poured a drop on the chair arm. It burnt a brown stain in the wood, eating its way through. The acid fumes made Irene blink.

'Pure nitric acid,' Hugo Dare murmured. 'It will eat through wood, metal — and flesh!'

'You swine,' Ernst raged. 'Leave the poor kid alone — haven't you done her enough harm, without torturing her?'

Muir struck the lieutenant across the face with his gun.

'Shut up, copper!' he snarled.

Dare dropped a tiny globule of the liquid on the back of Irene's hand. She screamed as it burned her skin and ate into the flesh. Her skin discoloured, turned brown where the acid spilled. She tried to get out of the chair, struggling against the ropes, crying with agony.

Dare gave her the pen again.

'Sign your confession,' he said. 'Sign it — or I'll give you the whole bottle. In your face!'

Irene shuddered. Ernst swore, and Muir hit him again. Dare raised the bottle to throw the contents in Irene's face.

'I'm no chemist,' he said easily. 'I can't be sure it will kill you. Certainly you'll be blinded — and no man will look on your face without shuddering. Do you want me to spoil your beauty — or will you sign?'

He made to throw the acid. Irene screamed in horror.

'No, no! Oh God, don't throw it! I'll sign — I'll sign!'

Dare put down the bottle. Irene Kline, with trembling fingers, scrawled her signature to the confession. She sobbed bitterly all the while.

Dare took the paper away from her, blotted it, placed it carefully in an inside pocket of his jacket. He picked up the bottle again.

'Just one more thing,' he purred. 'Where did Spain hide you? Tell me the name of the man who sheltered you from the police?'

Irene said: 'I won't tell you that. You can't make me tell you that.'

Paula laughed.

'She thinks you're kidding her. Give her the acid, Hugo — I want to hear her scream as it burns her eyes out!'

Hugo Dare raised the bottle again. His arm swung back.

'Who hid you, Irene? You've got till I count five — then I'll mar your beauty permanently. One . . . two . . . three . . . '

'I'll never tell you — never!'

Irene closed her eyes and waited. She began to shake with fear.

10

As Wang Lee and Hugo Dare went through the door behind an oriental curtain, out of the room, Woodroffe brought out Sam's .45 and moved towards him. The giant grinned at Sam and jerked the remaining needle from his face. Sam moaned as his flesh came away with the needle.

'I don't like coppers,' Woodroffe grunted. 'I'm gonna like this.'

He aimed the heavy gun at Sam's face. His finger curled about the trigger.

'I'm gonna blow your face off,' he said.

Sam sweated. He licked his lips, said:

'You're yellow right through, Woodroffe. If I had my hands free, I'd take you apart.'

Woodroffe guffawed. He flexed his muscles and boasted.

'You little runt, I could break you in pieces with one arm tied behind my back.'

'Well, why don't you? I'll tell you why — you're scared! You know that if you unstrapped me, I'd make a meal of you . . .'

Woodroffe didn't like that. His ugly face scowled.

'You wouldn't know what hit you, copper. One swipe with my fist would land you in the middle of next week!'

Sam jeered: 'Try it — go on, let me loose and try it!'

Woodroffe hesitated. He lowered his gun and stared at Sam.

'You trying to pull something?' he grunted suspiciously. 'It's a trick.'

Sam laughed derisively.

'Trick! How can I pull anything? You've a gun — I dare you to release me and prove your boasting. If you don't, I'll know you're scared. You figure you're the strong man around here — let's see you back up your words.'

Woodroffe took a long time to work it out. He hadn't much brain. Sam waited hopefully; he didn't know if he could beat the giant in a fight, but anything was better than being shot in cold blood. And he'd knock some of the swagger out of Woodroffe before the end came.

'You're yellow!' Sam jeered. 'You can only threaten a man who's tied down. You'd crawl in a corner to beg for mercy if I had my hands free.'

The insult got under Woodroffe's skin.

'We'll see,' he said grimly. 'All right, copper, if you want it the hard way — I'll turn you loose. Then I'll beat you to a pulp!'

Sam breathed a sigh of relief. The giant unfastened the straps and Sam swung himself off the table. He massaged his arms and legs to get his circulation going.

Woodroffe put his gun away. He said:

'This is it, copper. Say your prayers.'

He swung his fist into Sam's face. Sam cried out in agony as Woodroffe's knuckles smashed into his lacerated cheek. He rocked back on his heels, spun about and fell to the ground. Woodroffe kicked him brutally, and sneered:

'What are you lying down for, copper? You want me to shoot you now?'

Sam rolled across the floor and came up fighting. He slammed a left and a right to the giant's jaw. Woodroffe chuckled. He didn't move back; Sam's punches never disturbed his balance.

Woodroffe swung a hamlike fist at Sam's bare chest. It felt as if a steamhammer crashed against his ribs. Sam moaned; the giant hit him again on the place where Wang Lee had been pushing red-hot needles into him. The wounds opened up and blood ran down Sam's chest. The agony was excruciating; it sent him mad.

He leapt at Woodroffe, hurling his fists at him in a wild frenzy. The giant was forced to give ground under the ferocity of his attack, but Sam wasn't really hurting him. Woodroffe was too large and too tough to be hurt. Sam exhausted his attack and Woodroffe came forward again. He caught hold of Sam's arm and twisted it.

Sam brought up his knee sharply. Woodroffe grunted with pain and let go. Sam drove solid punches into his stomach, forcing him back. Woodroffe kicked out and his heavy boot caught Sam's shin. Sam's leg buckled under him;

he staggered; the giant kicked him into a sprawling heap.

Woodroffe said: 'Think you're tough, copper? When I've finished with you, you'll think you've been through the mangle!'

Sam dodged the giant's flailing boots and sprang upright. His breath was coming in choked sobs; his chest felt as if Wang Lee were still pushing needles into it; he knew he hadn't the strength to beat Woodroffe. He contented himself with pushing out his right in short jabs, preventing Woodroffe from getting at close quarters. He had to use his brain, beat the giant by cunning.

Woodroffe followed him as he backed round the room. He wanted to get his arms about Sam, to crush the life out of him in a rib-breaking bear-hug. Sam's eyes flickered about the room, searching for a weapon. He saw the coke brazier, and a steel poker standing beside it . . .

Sam moved closer to the brazier. Woodroffe lunged after him. Sam ducked under the giant's outspread arms and stuck out his foot. Woodroffe tripped and stumbled — fell heavily towards the brazier. He tried to save himself, too late — his face buried itself in the glowing coals and he screamed.

Sam grabbed the poker as Woodroffe staggered about the room, holding his face. The giant was crying with pain and his fingers clutched at his scorched and seared face where the skin had been burnt off. Sam hit him once, behind the head at the base of the skull. His neck broke with a sharp crack and he fell lifeless to the floor.

Sam Spain leant heavily against the wall, gasping for air. The fight had taken a lot out of him and, following on top of Wang Lee's torture, left him weak. He wanted to rest, but knew the danger of doing so. He dropped to his knees and went through Woodroffe's pockets.

There was no sound, but a draught on his neck warned Sam that someone had entered the room. The noise of the struggle had been overheard. Sam grabbed for the .45 automatic in Woodroffe's pocket and rolled sideways.

A yellow face gleamed in the lamplight

and a clawed hand held a curved knife. It was the servant who had let Sam in on his first visit to the House of the Seven Moons. Sam brought up his gun and squeezed the trigger in one movement.

The Chinese had no chance to throw the knife before Sam's slug crashed into his face. The man went backwards and made a heap in the doorway.

Sam pulled the body aside and stepped through into a dark passage. He listened, gun in hand, waiting to hear if anyone else was coming. There was no further sound.

Sam groped his way along the passage, up a short flight of stairs. He found a door and, inside, a light switch. He used it to flood the room with light and found himself in a storeroom. There were packing cases stacked round the walls, reaching from floor to ceiling. One of the cases had been opened and a white powder lay exposed. Sam smelled it. Heroin!

Sam whistled. There was enough of the drug to supply San Francisco for a year. He began to understand why Hugo Dare wanted to get Irene Kline sentenced for Bartlett's murder; if he were behind Wang Lee's dope racket, he couldn't afford to allow the investigation to drag on. Dare's political regime would end the minute his name was connected with such a vicious practice.

He remembered what Dare had said about moving the 'stuff' to the 400 Club, and he began to piece together the parts of the jigsaw. Hugo Dare bought the heroin south of the border; it was shipped to California and smuggled through Wang Lee's house, to be distributed at the night club. Muir was in it, too.

Maybe Bartlett had been an under-cover man for the Narcotics Detail; he'd got on to Dare's trail and had been bumped off. Irene Kline had been dragged in to cover up . . .

Sam didn't have time for further thought. A door opened and Wang Lee came into the storeroom with two Chinese. Wang Lee saw Sam and snapped an order. A shot boomed across the room; plaster chipped from the wall over Sam's head as he ducked behind a packing case.

He shot out the light and worked his way round the wall.

Wang Lee's voice came through the darkness:

'Surrender, Master of Spies — you cannot escape!'

Sam snapped a shot at the voice. Red tongues of answering fire lanced the gloom. The shots echoed loudly and the smell of cordite was acrid in the confined space. One of the Chinese became excited and loosed off his gun. Sam pinpointed the stabbing crimson flame and fired once. He heard the man groan; the shooting stopped.

Sam changed his position. He waited. Wang Lee and one Chinese remained — and he had four shells left. He couldn't afford to miss . . .

The black silence grew oppressive. Sam felt in his pocket for a coin, threw it across the room. It clinked on the ground and a red flame blazed out. Sam fired a couple of inches to the right of the tell-tale flash — and hit the second Chinese. He heard the man's gun clatter on the floor.

Sam smiled in the darkness. He was alone with Wang Lee now; that was how he liked it. He remembered how the Chinese had tortured him, and called:

'It's between the two of us, Wang Lee. I'm coming after you!'

Sam crawled forward, judging where the door would be in the blackness. Wang Lee must be somewhere near the door, so Sam headed that way. He couldn't hear the Chinese moving, couldn't even pick up the sound of breathing. Then a blinding light stabbed out of the gloom, hitting Sam between the eyes, blinding him.

He had almost walked into Wang Lee without knowing it — and the Chinese had turned a flashlight on his face, dazzling him. Sam glimpsed an ivory mask, a long waxed moustache and glittering eyes — caught the flash of a knife blade as Wang Lee hissed:

'Die, Prince of Detectives!'

Sam knocked the steel blade aside; it missed his shoulder by a hair's breadth as it sliced down. He pushed the muzzle of his automatic into Wang Lee's belly and squeezed the trigger.

The shot was muffled: the flash hidden. The gun kicked back in Sam's hand.

Wang Lee shuddered as the heavy slug tore at his intestines; he twisted, and the torch fell from his fingers. He folded his hands across his middle, pressing back the flow of blood, and sank to the ground. He lay there moaning, dying slowly . . .

Sam picked up the torch and turned it on him. Wang Lee's blue robe was stained red under his long fingernails and the stain spread slowly across the floor. Sam left him there, moaning and writhing in agony. Wang Lee would die before help reached him, but he wouldn't die easily. Sam didn't let that worry him.

Beyond the door of the storeroom, another passage stretched through the House of the Seven Moons. With the flashlight to guide him, Sam travelled quickly. There seemed to be no-one else in the house. Sam went up another flight of stairs, to the room where he had first met Wang Lee.

Here, he found his clothes — and the two boxes of shells in his coat pocket. He loaded the automatic, ready for action again. He pulled his shirt over his head, tucked it into the waistband of his slacks. The shirt stuck to the matted blood on his chest. He slipped into his coat and left the room.

Sam went through a maze of passages to the front door, let himself out onto the street. He was surprised when bright sunlight hit his eyes. So long had he been in the dark that he'd lost track of time: it must be about noon, he guessed.

There was a 'phone booth on the corner of Pagoda Place and Sam used it. He rang Joey first.

'I posted your letter,' Joey started, but Sam cut him short.

'Never mind that now. Things have been moving fast — I reckon I'll have this case sewn up before Ernst gets my letter. I want you to go over to the 400 Club and take care of Muir. Put him somewhere safe. I'm going out to Dare's house. They've got Irene there and I'm scared for her. I may need a little gun help, so follow on as soon as you've put Muir out of the way.'

Joey said: 'Okay, Sam, I'll see you at Dare's place.'

Sam dialled another number. A voice said:

'Police Headquarters, Narcotics Detail.'

Sam said: 'Take down this address. House of the Seven Moons, Pagoda Place.'

'Got it,' replied the cop. 'What about it?'

Sam said: 'You'll find five corpses there — and a storeroom full of heroin.'

He replaced the receiver and left the booth. He was weak and hungry, but his thoughts were only of Irene. He had to get to her fast; she needed help. It was only now that Sam realized how much she had come to mean to him in the past hectic hours.

A cab idled by. Sam hailed it and piled in the back.

'Skyline Boulevard,' he snapped at the driver.

Gears meshed; the cab darted forward, gathering speed. It travelled west, along Clay Street to Lafayette Park, swung south down Gough Street.

'Step on it,' Sam rapped. 'I'm in a hurry.'

The cab moved into Market Street and picked up Portola Drive. Sam fretted with impatience. He was badly worried about Irene; he didn't like to think what Hugo Dare might be doing to her. He gripped his automatic and promised himself that Dare would never again bother anyone.

They passed Twin Peaks and shot the traffic lights at the junction of Woodside and O'Shaughnessy. The driver grumbled:

'I can't go any faster, bud. What's the hurry — somebody dying?'

Sam thought grimly: that might be too near the truth.

It was hot in the cab and the swaying motion did things to Sam's empty stomach. His chest throbbed and burned and his head grew muzzy. He told himself he had to hang on — but it was no use. His body had taken too much. His eyes closed and he slumped forward into unconsciousness.

11

Joey put down the telephone with a sigh of relief. He'd been worried about Sam and it was good to hear his voice again. It was even better to hear that Dare was going to get what was coming to him — and soon.

He smiled a little. He'd seen how it was between Sam and the girl when they'd first arrived at his café. Sam's anxiety made it clear that he, too, realized he was in love with Irene. Joey frowned. It wasn't so good that Dare had the girl at his house, but Sam would attend to that.

Joey waddled to his room and opened a drawer. He took out a second .45 automatic, similar to the one he'd given Sam, and loaded it. He put the gun in his pocket and locked up the café.

He walked round the corner to the garage, wishing he wasn't quite so fat. He'd have liked to be able to move quicker. His bald head glistened with perspiration by the time he reached the garage. He waggled his eyebrows at the mechanic, and said:

'I want to hire a fast car.'

The mechanic seemed suspicious.

'What happened to the Humber ? You wreck it?'

'I loaned it to a friend of mine,' Joey said. 'Don't worry, you'll be paid. And I'm in a hurry.'

He got a car, a black Packard, and settled behind the wheel. The automatic made a comforting bulge in his pocket. Joey liked the idea of going gunning for crooks; he remembered when his café had been threatened by mobsters operating a protection racket. It had been Sam who had helped him then. Joey would do anything to help Sam — and if he could take a crack at the crooks who spoilt San Francisco at the same time, so much the better.

He drove the Packard along the waterfront, heading north, and turned onto Third Street. He travelled along the broad concrete of the Embarcadero with his foot on the accelerator. On his right, jetties stuck out into the bay. He passed under the San Francisco-Oakland Bay Bridge and past Ferry building at the bottom of Market Street.

Jocy enjoyed the prospect of dealing with Ambrose Muir. He hoped the night club manager would put up a fight, thinking how nice it would be to use the .45 on him. At Bay Street, the Packard swung left to pick up Marina Boulevard. He found the 400 Club opposite the park, stopped the car and went into the foyer of the club.

There didn't seem to be anyone around. Joey shouted:

'Anyone at home ? I'm looking for the manager.'

A cleaner came out from behind the bar and glared at Joey.

'Muir's out,' the cleaner said briefly.

Joey hadn't thought of that before. He thought of it now.

'Where?' he demanded.

The cleaner shrugged.

'How would I know? Muir doesn't take me into his confidence.'

'There must be someone around who

knows where he is,' Joey said. 'It's urgent.'

Just how urgent, Ambrose Muir would find out when Joey stuck a gun in his ribs and gave him marching orders. But he hadn't located Muir yet.

The cleaner said: 'Usually, Cabot or Woodroffe are around — they'd know where the boss is. But I haven't seen them either. They're all out someplace.'

Joey decided that wasn't so good. Sam wanted Muir out of the way and he couldn't find the night club manager. That worried Joey. Sam might be running into trouble at Dare's place and he wanted to get out there fast.

Joey went out to the Packard, determined to go straight to Hugo Dare's house and back up Sam's play; Muir would have to wait till later. It wasn't till he was driving along the Lincoln Boulevard, that Joey suddenly realized Muir might be visiting Dare. In which case, Sam would have his hands full.

Joey cursed, and stamped on the accelerator. The Packard picked up El Camino Del Mar and swept through Lincoln Park, onto Point Lobos Avenue.

He climbed Sutro Heights and passed Cliff House. Below, the Pacific stretched blue and silver to the horizon and seals basked in the sun on the famous Seal Rocks.

But Joey was in no mood to watch seals; Sam might need him in a hurry. The Packard roared along the Great Highway, past Playland and the Golden Gate Park, to pick up Skyline Boulevard, by the Fleish-hacker Zoo. Lake Merced appeared on his left, and, beyond the sand dunes, Hugo Dare's residence.

Joey turned into the drive and went up to the house. He stopped the car and get out, gun in hand. He didn't bother with the front door. There was a French window open on the veranda; he used that.

He passed through an empty room, to a passage way. There was no-one about as Joey came to the tiled hall and looked up the curving stairway. He was wondering how to find Sam when he heard the scream. A girl's scream.

Joey went upstairs fast. He saw the oak doors and went through as Irene said:

'I'll never tell you — never!'

Joey saw Dare's arm move to throw the acid in her face. He said:

'Stop that!'

Hugo Dare turned. He lowered his arm as he saw Joey's automatic pointing at him. He set the bottle down, very carefully, on the table and replaced the stopper.

Joey moved into the room, looking for Sam. He recognized Irene. The others he didn't know, but he guessed their names easily. Hugo Dare, Muir, Paula, and a butler. He couldn't guess who the lanky man was, tied in another chair, opposite Irene.

Joey said: 'It would be a good idea if no-one moved — my trigger finger's nervous.'

The lanky man said: 'I'm Lieutenant Ernst, Homicide. Cut me loose and I'll take over.'

Joey hesitated. He knew Sam had been framed and was wanted by the police: he wasn't sure if Sam had managed to clear himself yet.

'Where's Sam' he asked.

Irene sobbed.

'He's dead, Joey. Hugo killed him and threw his body in the bay.'

Joey laughed.

'Sam isn't so easy to kill as that. I was talking to him on the 'phone not so long ago.'

Dare's face paled. Irene stopped crying; her eyes shone.

Joey said: 'Sam should be here by now.'

He moved towards Irene, intending to free her. He kept his gun trained on Hugo Dare. Muir and the butler didn't feel like risking a .45 slug. It was Paula who tricked Joey.

She was standing just behind the butler with a glass of whisky in her hand. Maybe she thought Joey wouldn't shoot a woman. She gave the butler a push so that he fell between her and Joey's gun — then threw the glass.

Joey shot the butler through the heart. Before he could move, the glass struck his face. Whisky splashed in his eyes, blinding him, and he staggered back.

Ernst shouted: 'Look out — '

Hugo Dare sprang forward, drawing his

own gun. He slammed down his gun on Joey's hand. Joey dropped his .45 with a cry of pain and held his hand. Dare hit him in the face, knocking him sprawling on the floor, and Muir scooped up the automatic.

'Nice work, Paula,' Hugo Dare said, smiling.

He lit a fresh cigar and looked down at Joey.

'I guess we know who hid the girl now,' he said. 'That makes everything fine.'

'Except for Sam Spain,' Muir pointed out.

Dare frowned.

'Yeah, except for Spain.'

He picked up a telephone and rang the house in Pagoda Place. The voice that answered was clean cut and official.

'San Francisco Police, Narcotics Detail.'

Dare replaced the receiver without speaking. He turned to the night club manager.

'Something's gone wrong — the cops are at Wang Lee's.'

Muir began to curse. He was badly shaken.

'It's Spain,' he said. 'He's ruined everything!'

Joey crawled off the floor, holding his bleeding face.

'Sam will get you rats,' he spat.

Muir hit the fat man in the face. He hit him again as Joey swore at him.

Ernst said: 'You guys had better cut and run. Sam's gonna be plenty mad when he learns how you've treated the girl. He's liable to start throwing lead as he comes through the door.'

That reminded Paula of Irene. The blonde wanted to spoil her features. She picked up the acid bottle, and said:

'Watch me, Hugo.'

Dare grabbed her arm, forcing her to put down the bottle.

'Not yet, Paula. The girl stays alive till we've got Spain — she's the bait we'll use to trap him. While we've got her alive, he'll come to us — and that simplifies matters.'

Muir's face was white. He began to whine.

'Let's get out of here, Hugo. If the cops are at Wang Lee's, they'll be on to the club, then here. And I don't fancy facing Spain — '

'Shut up!' Dare snapped. 'We're staying put. There's no lead from Chinatown to us. The only man who has anything on us is Spain — and as soon as he comes here, we'll finish him. Then we're in the clear.'

Paula said: 'That's sense, Ambrose. If we run now, we lose everything. If we get Spain, there's nothing to worry about.' She turned to Hugo. 'Afterwards — can I have the girl to play with?'

Dare chuckled.

'How you dames love each other! You're a bitch, Paula — but you can have the pleasure of killing her.'

Muir levelled his gun at Joey.

'There's no need for this fat pig to live any longer — nor the copper.'

Dare shook his head.

'Not here,' he said, pointing to the butler. 'We've already one body to get rid of. Maybe we'll kill them with Spain's gun — that'll seal off a few loose ends. Remember, we've got to put all the blame on the girl and Spain.'

Irene sobbed:

'Sam will beat you. You thought you'd killed him before — he'll get you.'

Paula hit her across the mouth, shutting her up. Muir tied Joey's hands.

'Lock them up for the present,' Hugo Dare said. 'In separate rooms. Then we'll prepare a reception committee for Spain.'

They took the lieutenant first. He went without a struggle. They came back for Joey.

'Don't worry, Irene,' Joey said, as they took him through the door. 'Sam can look after himself.'

But as they locked him in a dark cellar, he wondered: Where was Sam Spain ?

12

Sam opened his eyes to a whitewashed wall. The room was small and he was lying on a couch. There was a man in a white coat, washing his hands at a basin — a doctor.

Sam sat up and discovered that his bloodstained shirt had been stripped off. His chest had been bandaged and he felt a lot better. Then he remembered Irene, and where she was, and he knew he had to go places in a hurry.

'Hi, doc,' he said, swinging his feet to the floor and testing his legs. 'How long have I been out?'

The doctor turned, frowning.

'Get back on the couch. You're in no condition to walk around.'

Sam's legs supported him but he wasn't feeling as strong as he would have liked. But he couldn't wait — he had to get to Dare's place fast. He repeated:

'How long was I unconscious?'

'Two hours,' the doctor said. 'And lay down — you're a very sick man.'

Sam's grey eyes smiled. He picked up his coat and put it on. He didn't bother with his shirt, but buttoned his coat over the bandages. He felt the weight of the automatic in his pocket. All he wanted now was a car . . .

'I don't know how you got those wounds,' the doctor said, 'but it looks like a job for the police. A cab driver brought you in, said you'd passed out in his cab.'

Sam nodded. He suddenly remembered that he'd told Joey to meet him at Hugo Dare's house, after dealing with Muir. He hoped Joey hadn't run into trouble.

'Lay down,' the doctor rapped. 'You're my patient — and I say you're not going anywhere.'

'You're wrong, doc,' Sam said. He showed his gun to the doctor, who stepped back. 'No-one argues with this kind of persuasion.'

He moved towards the door.

'I'll call the police,' the doctor threatened.

'Do that — and tell them to call at Dare's residence on Skyline Boulevard. I'll have some new corpses lined up, waiting for them.'

Sam went through the door, called back:

'Thanks for patching me up, doc. I'll see you later — maybe.'

Outside the doctor's house, a car stood in the roadway. Sam wasn't bothered who owned the car; he was in a hurry. He got in and drove off. The doc's place was on Vicente Street; Sam headed out to get on Portola Drive. He travelled fast, southwest to the Junipero Serro Boulevard, then south. He swung right and kept going till he reached Lake Merced.

His foot was hard down on the accelerator as he went round the edge of the lake. He turned off the boulevard and headed across the sand dunes, towards Sky Line and the Pacific — towards Dare's house.

The car jumped about on the dunes, wheels spinning madly in the sand. The engine roared in protest as the car churned sand and scrub, moving side-ways like a crazy thing. Sam bounced in the seat, gritting his teeth. He kept his foot down on the accelerator and spun the wheel madly.

He reached the high wall bordering the grounds of Dare's house and stopped under the wall. He got out, climbed on top of the car. He could look out over the grounds, through the trees to the house. It was very quiet.

Sam took out his automatic and checked it quickly. Then he vaulted the wall, landing on his feet on soft grass. He trotted between the trees, moving up to a door at the rear of the house.

He sprinted across an open stretch of lawn to reach the door. No shots came. It seemed that no-one saw him. The house might have been deserted.

Sam prayed that Irene was still alive. And Joey — Joey must be inside the house somewhere. The fat man must surely have reached here before Sam. Sam Spain pushed open the door and went in. He decided it was too quiet.

Irene Kline shivered in the darkness. Her prison was a cellar below the house, a cellar with bare stone walls and a massive oak door. There was no light and the only air came through a square metal grille high in one wall.

They hadn't bothered to tie her up. With steel bolts on the outside of the door, escape was impossible. She measured her cell again, four paces through the blackness one way, five the other. There was no furniture.

The floor was damp and cold so she had to stand all the time. The stone walls were running with moisture and cobwebs brushed her hair. She shuddered as a spider crawled down her face. Her legs ached, but the only way she could rest was by leaning against the oak door. She soon got tired of that.

She felt her way round the cellar again. The walls were unbroken, cold and hard under her hands. There was no way out, except through the door — and that was bolted on the other side.

It seemed days since she had been locked in the dark; she had no idea of the actual passage of time. She thought about Sam, and was afraid for him. She knew she loved him — and that, because of her, he was walking into a trap. Tears rolled down her cheeks.

Then she thought of Hugo Dare, and stopped crying. She paced the stone floor, five steps to the wall, five back again. She went on pacing through the darkness, thinking of Hugo and working herself into a fury.

He'd told her he loved her, had promised to marry her. Then he'd laughed in her face, scorned her . . . Irene hated him. Her face twisted in harsh lines and she began to mutter to herself. She wanted to kill him.

He'd called her a slut, said that no man could want her. Irene's hands twisted in tight knots. Hatred surged through her body, driving her mad. If only she could get her hands on him . . .

A drum beat inside her head. She grew rigid with the desire to kill. Her face was a mask of bitterness and she dug her nails into the palms of her hands. The beating in her head throbbed louder. Vengeance!

Her pacing quickened with her raging emotions. She went round and round the cellar, glaring into the darkness, talking herself into an insane passion. The drum beat on . . . kill Hugo . . . kill Hugo . . . kill Hugo!

Her face hurt where she had been struck; her stomach ached where Paula had hit her; the back of her hand itched where the acid had burned a brown stain. She remembered how Dare had been about to throw the acid in her face. She shuddered with the horror of the memory. Hugo had a lot to answer for.

A light came on in the cellar. Irene stopped pacing and looked up at the stone ceiling. An electric light bulb gleamed, starkly revealing the bare stone walls, the trickle of moisture. The light was controlled from the passage outside — someone was at the door, coming in. Irene faced the door, her face set. If it was Hugo, she'd kill him — nothing could stop her.

Nothing happened for what seemed hours. It could only have been a couple of minutes; then she heard the sound of bolts being withdrawn. The door opened outwards, slowly. A voice said:

'I've a gun in my hand. If you try to escape, I'll shoot you down.'

Irene recognized Paula's voice. The blonde moved into view.

'Back against the wall,' Paula said sharply.

Irene went back. She didn't doubt that the blonde would kill her if she didn't obey — and she wanted to go on living. It was important that she go on living until she got to Hugo Dare.

Paula came into the cellar, closing the door behind her. She was dressed in a crimson gown and her platinum hair glistened in the electric light. She swayed towards Irene, holding her revolver low, pointing it at Irene's stomach. She was smoking a cigarette through a long holder.

Irene didn't have to ask why the blonde had come. She could see the reason in her eyes; the gleam of sadistic pleasure. Paula had come to torment her . . .

'You look a wreck,' Paula sneered. 'You dirty little slut, you think you can take Hugo away from me — *me*?'

The blonde was a beautiful, sensuous animal. She stared at Irene pityingly, at her ragged dyed hair and soiled blouse, her torn skirt and cheap stockings, her down-at-heel shoes.

Irene didn't say anything. She backed to the wall, watching the blonde. The door was unlocked; if she could get past Paula . . .

'Try it,' the blonde said viciously. 'Try it and I'll fill you full of lead!'

She jabbed the muzzle of her revolver hard into Irene's stomach, tightening her finger about the trigger. Irene winced. Paula blew tobacco smoke in her eyes, making them water.

'Hugo and Ambrose are upstairs,' the blonde said, 'waiting for Spain to show up. They've got three gunmen with them. Spain's gonna get it good when he sticks his nose in. Like the idea?'

Irene's face went white. Sam didn't have a chance. She pressed back against the wall, her fingers clawing the damp stone.

'I thought you'd be interested in exactly how Spain is going to die,' Paula said softly. 'And what's going to happen to you, afterwards.'

Irene's outstretched fingers discovered a loose stone in the cellar wall She worked at the stone, trying to free it. She kept her eyes fixed on the blonde's face, hoping her groping fingers wouldn't be noticed. She said:

'Sam will trick you. He'll save me — '

Paula laughed.

'Spain will be full of lead before he knows what hit him. But you — you won't die so easily. Hugo has promised *I* can have you to play with . . . now that he has your confession, there's no need to turn you over to the cops.'

Irene had the loose stone half out of the wall. She tried to work her fingers round it, to get a good grip.

Paula said: 'Spain will die quickly, but you — you'll be a long time dying. You know what I'm gonna do? I'm going to use the acid on you!'

She blew more smoke in Irene's eyes. Irene almost had the stone now; she was almost ready to strike.

Paula said: 'I'm going to strip you and let the acid drip over you, slowly, drop by drop, till your flesh is eaten away. And I'm gonna enjoy every minute of it!'

She leaned forward, digging the revolver into Irene's stomach. Her left hand gripped Irene's blouse, tore it down, exposing white flesh. She took the cigarette from its holder and rammed the glowing stub into the hollow of Irene's throat. Irene screamed madly with pain, twisting sideways . . . her hand came up, with the stone in it, smashed into the blonde's mouth.

Paula moaned. Her revolver exploded like a cannon in the smallness of the stone cell. Irene felt the slug tear at her thigh — her leg dragged uselessly and she fell on top of the blonde. She hit Paula again with the stone, knocking the gun from her hand. It slithered across the damp floor to the wall.

Irene tried to reach the gun. Paula grabbed her hair and jerked brutally. Her mouth hurt and blood ran down her face;

she wanted to kill Irene for hitting her. She gouged Irene's face with her fingernails, swearing horribly.

Irene rolled over, dragging Paula with her on the stone floor. She tore at the blonde's crimson gown, splitting it open. She pummelled Paula's lovely body till it bled in a dozen places. They rolled on the ground, fighting and spitting like wild cats.

Paula started to shout for help. Irene hurled the stone at her mouth, smashing her teeth. Paula sobbed piteously and tried to cover her face. Irene, demented with pain and hatred, beat the blonde's face to a pulp. She went on hitting her, long after Paula had stopped moaning, had stopped moving . . .

Irene, tired and weak, climbed to her feet. She looked down at the dead body of Paula with a grim smile of satisfaction. She dropped the stone to the floor.

Blood trickled down Irene's leg. The bullet from Paula's gun had gone right through her thigh, leaving a flesh wound. She tore a strip from the dead girl's dress and bound the wound. She picked up

Paula's revolver and stepped through the door to a passage. Her leg dragged a little, but she went on, up the stairs.

No-one had heard the fight in the cellar. Irene reached the ground floor and saw three men waiting in the hall. She hid behind a pillar, waiting for them to go away. Then she moved up the stairs, gun in hand.

Killing Paula had roused something in her; she wanted to get at Hugo Dare. Her face was a grim mask of hatred as she went up the stairs, her injured leg dragging heavily. The drum beat in her head again . . . revenge!

Revenge on the man who had scorned her. This time she was going to settle with Hugo — this time she was really going to kill him. Nothing could stop her now.

The desire to kill flamed through her like a raging fury. Her breath came quickly; her body was rigid, tensed with expectancy. Her eyes gleamed with a mad light and there was only one thought in her head . . . kill!

She reached the top of the stairs and moved along the passage to double oak doors. Hugo would be there. She held the revolver tightly as she padded forward, eager for the kill.

She shook with the urgency of her desire for vengeance. This was what she had been waiting for, living for. Her big moment had come. All of Hugo Dare's treachery flashed through her head as she stepped through the oak doors — Irene Kline was about to kill a man.

13

It was much too quiet in Hugo Dare's house. Sam went along the passage, his automatic ready for action. He was guessing that Joey had made his play and been caught — or killed. Dare would be expecting him now. The quietness was a part of the trap.

Sam remembered the lay-out of the house. He thought of the wide hallway, the curving stairs, and smiled. That was where they'd try to get him. It was open and there was no cover for him as he went up the stairs. And he had to go up because Dare would be waiting for him at the top.

Sam didn't want to hurry; he knew he'd better go carefully, spot the trap and spring it first. But he was worried about Irene — even seconds might count if Dare was set to kill her.

He had to force the pace, open the action himself. He had to strike first, and hardest, not giving Dare time to regroup his men. If he failed, Irene would die. Joey, too.

Sam came abreast of the hallway, moving stealthily, taking cover behind a stone pedestal. His eyes raked the shadows on the far side of the hall, spotted a movement at the top of the curving staircase. He brought up his gun, fired at the movement, and dropped flat on his face.

The man on the balcony staggered, held his hands to his chest, and crashed down the stairs. A hail of bullets swept the hallway. Somebody was using a tommy gun. The woodwork above Sam's head splintered as the gun sprayed a deadly arc of lead. Sam spotted the man, a man with a hatchet face and a sub-machine gun in his arms. The man crouched behind an upright supporting the staircase.

Sam wriggled forward on his stomach, bringing his automatic to bear on the hatchet man. He sighted the .45 carefully, squeezed the trigger. A shot blasted out, echoing noisily; red flame stabbed across the hallway. The heavy slug caught the man in the shoulder and he dropped his tommy gun, staggering. Sam fired again, hit him in the chest. The hatchet man was dead before he hit the floor.

Another gun boomed. A splinter of wood lashed Sam's face. He rolled to cover, trying to spot the third gunman. There was a moment of silence while Sam and the gunman watched for the telltale movement that would give the other's position away.

Sam crawled into a kneeling position, his automatic ready to blast sudden death. He was sure the gunman was across the hall, but he couldn't spot him. A shot rang out. Sam felt the bullet whine past his head. He dropped flat, cursing. That shot had come from the top of the stairs. He glanced up and saw Ambrose Muir on the balcony.

Muir ducked hastily as Sam winged a slug upwards. That gave away Sam's position; the hatchet man across the hall opened up, spraying lead at Sam. A flying shell grazed Sam's head, drawing a trickle of blood and half-stunning him. He lay still, gripping his automatic and waiting for the hatchet man to come out for the kill. But the gunman was wary; he kept under cover, uncertain of the damage he had inflicted.

Sam rolled a coin along the floor. A shot crashed out — and a slug caught the coin in the centre, drilling a hole through it. Sam sweated. That was first-class shooting. He pinpointed the direction from which the shot had come, and fired.

His .45 shell chipped an ornamental vase, but did no other damage. The gunman exchanged another shot with him. Muir fired from the balcony, but his shot went wide; he hadn't seen Sam take up a fresh position.

Sam grew impatient of the long-drawn out battle; he couldn't afford to wait, not with Irene in danger. Reloading his automatic, he decided to gamble on the speed of his gun-hand. He stepped from cover, out into the open. He saw a hand come from behind a pillar, a revolver point at him. Sam shot first; his slug buried itself in the hatchet man's hand and a revolver skidded across the floor.

Muir fired from the balcony. Sam ducked, fired back. Muir ran for cover.

The hatchet man went after his gun; he knew Sam would shoot him down in cold blood — he had to have his revolver. His hand grasped the gun as Sam's .45 spoke.

A heavy shell caught the gunman square between the eyes. His jaw dropped and blood poured down his face. He died so quickly that he never knew anything about it.

Sam stood motionless, in the centre of the hall. His eyes flickered round, watching for the movement that never came. Three gunmen lay still in death; it had been a nice trap but it hadn't worked.

Sam breathed easier; there were no more hidden guns to blast him down. He started up the stairs, watching for Ambrose Muir. The night club manager scared easily. He fired wildly, missing Sam by yards, and ran.

Sam winged a shot after him, but Muir was travelling too fast. Ambrose Muir ran along the passage at the top of the stairs, shouting:

'Hugo! It's Spain! He's coming after you!'

Sam went on up, gun in hand. He

stopped, the blood freezing in his veins as he heard a ghastly shriek from the room at the top of the stairs. He'd never heard anything so terrifying in his life. The screaming went on and on, then tailed off into a pitiful blubbering.

Sam started to run. His face was grim, his trigger finger jumpy. He prayed that it couldn't be Irene who made that awful noise. He sprinted along the passage to the double oak doors.

He heard a gun-shot — but the moaning still went on. Sam Spain passed through oak doors, into the room.

★ ★ ★

Hugo Dare was alone in the room when Irene walked in. He was seated on the divan, smoking a cigar and looking pleased with himself. Without looking up, he said:

'All set, Ambrose? I guess Spain — '

Irene said: 'It isn't Ambrose, Hugo.'

Dare came to his feet, turning quickly. He gasped, made a movement towards his gun — stopped as he saw Irene's revolver pointing at him, the look on her face.

'I'm going to kill you,' she said.

Dare backed away. She was mad, he could tell that from the light in her eyes. She was a terrifying spectacle with blood streaming down her face, one leg dragging behind her. Her blouse was torn and there was a cigarette burn on her throat.

Dare mumbled: 'Irene — please . . . '

She laughed insanely, moving towards him. Her face was a mask of hatred, the hand holding her gun, white and stiff.

'You shouldn't have scorned me, Hugo,' she whispered. 'You shouldn't have said you loved me, then turned me down. You shouldn't have laughed — no girl can stand *that*.'

Dare began to shake. His face paled, his lantern jaw dropped, his dark eyes held a silent appeal. He knew she would kill him; the expression on her face left no room for doubt on that score.

He started to speak, but his voice was a dry croak.

'For God's sake, Irene — don't shoot! Give me a chance — I'll make it up to you somehow.'

She moved nearer, quivering with hatred. A drum beat and throbbed inside her head . . . kill . . . kill . . . kill!

'I'm a slut,' she said flatly. 'Remember, Hugo — you called me a slut. You preferred your fancy woman — well, you wouldn't like her now. I left her in the cellar — dead!'

'You were right to kill her,' Dare said quickly. He was playing for time. Muir was due any minute — if he could stall her . . . 'Paula was no good. I was wrong about you, Irene — '

Her maniacal laughter chilled his blood. She was breathing too fast, like a woman filled with dope. Her eyes flashed with wild fury. Her body tensed, became rigid, as she lowered the revolver, directing its muzzle at his stomach. He saw her finger tighten about the trigger . . .

Dare grabbed for his gun, knowing he had no other chance. Irene laughed, but didn't shoot. She struck his face with her revolver. Dare cried out, dropped the gun to hold his face. Irene kicked his gun away. He was unarmed now; she could do anything she liked with him.

She hit him again, knocking him back on the divan. Her eyes spotted the bottle of nitric acid on the table, and she smiled. It was the sort of smile a cat wears when about to pounce on a helpless mouse.

'Hugo,' she said softly, 'you were going to throw acid in my face. I wonder how you'll like it? You know what I'm going to do, don't you, Hugo?'

Sweat poured down Dare's face. He croaked:

'No — don't! Irene, for God's sake . . . '

She removed the stopper from the bottle of acid, picked it up. Acrid fumes came from the colourless liquid. Dare began to shake with helpless terror. He'd never seen such fury and hatred in a girl's face before. He'd never been so frightened that his legs turned to jelly and he couldn't move, that his voice refused to function and only a low whining came out.

'No — no! Have pity — '

A fusillade of shots rang out from downstairs. Irene paused, lowering the bottle. She wondered, vaguely, what was happening. Dare found his voice: he said, urgently:

'That's Spain — my men will kill him. You don't want that, do you? Let me go and tell them to stop shooting.'

Irene said: 'Stand still, Hugo. I'm going to kill you!'

Dare pleaded: 'Don't throw the acid, Irene — don't — '

She stood over him, one leg dragging behind her. The shooting meant nothing to her; she'd forgotten that Sam existed. She was aware only of the incessant throbbing inside her head, the throbbing that went: kill . . . kill . . . kill!

Nothing else mattered. Only the beating in her head and the crawling wreck of a man at her feet. His face looked up, white and lined with terror. He whined:

'Don't — My God, don't — '

Irene laughed mercilessly. She said:

'You shouldn't have scorned me, Hugo. You shouldn't have thrown away my love, laughed at me. This is it, Hugo . . . the end — for you!'

She drew back her arm and, in one lightning movement, threw the contents of the bottle full in his face. The acid came out in a silent, colourless stream. It splashed into Dare's eyes, blinding him; ran into his mouth and burned his tongue; trickled down his face, off his lantern jaw to eat away his clothes.

He shrieked as the acid stung his flesh; went on screaming as the skin peeled from his face. He couldn't see any more; his eyes were sightless burning orbs. He staggered like a drunken man, holding his face with his hands and shrieking with the searing agony. The acid ate into his face, burning away his features, leaving raw flesh, brown and discoloured.

Irene dropped the empty bottle and laughed as Hugo Dare writhed on the floor, his screaming trailing off into a child-ish blubbering. She was still laughing when Ambrose Muir ran through the doorway. He saw Irene and what she'd done to Hugo Dare. He brought up his gun and fired.

Irene felt red-hot pain shoot through her shoulder. She swayed, toppled to the ground . . . Muir raised his gun to finish her. And Sam Spain came into the room.

A lead slug spat from Sam's .45 auto-matic, catching Muir full in the chest. He spun round and crashed to the floor as the shell reached his heart. He didn't move from the tangled heap he made on the carpet. Ambrose Muir was dead.

Sam bent over Irene. She was still conscious. She murmured:

'I got him, Sam . . . I got him!'

Then she passed out. Sam inspected her wounds. A flesh wound in the thigh, another in the shoulder. She'd live, all right. His sigh of relief was audible.

Hugo Dare was still moaning softly. Sam looked at him, and shuddered. The acid had eaten away all his face; there was just a mass of raw flesh, horribly discoloured. He was dying, slowly and painfully.

Sam raised his gun and fired into Dare's heart. The faceless body jerked once, then slumped into death. Hugo Dare had finished with politics and murder and everything else.

Sam turned away, his stomach vomiting. Dare wasn't a pretty sight. Sam glanced at Irene and his grey eyes smiled bleakly.

He said: 'Hell hath no fury . . . like a woman scorned!'

Then the cops arrived to take over.

Sam wasn't in hospital long; long enough for Lieutenant Ernst to call.

Ernst said: 'Everything's cleaned up, Sam. You don't have to worry about knocking off a few thugs. And I burned the confession that Dare forced Miss Kline to sign.'

He lit two cigarettes, passed one to Sam. Sam inhaled gratefully.

Ernst went on: 'The D.A.'s pleased with the way you've handled things. I guess he's relieved to have political pressure taken off him. We pinched the whole of Wang Lee's store of heroin, and that at the 400 Club. They had a nice racket there. I guess you're due for a reward from the City Hall, Sam.'

Sam grinned.

'I think I've a reward coming from a different quarter!'

Ernst knew what he meant. He chuckled.

'Best of luck, Sam, and be careful how you treat her. I wouldn't want to find you with no face one day!'

Sam said: 'I'll use velvet gloves with all dames from now on — I've learnt a lot about the female of the species on this case. But tell me; Bartlett — was he an undercover man for Narcotics?'

Ernst shook his head.

'Nothing like that. Bartlett was a heroin user himself. Then he got onto a lead between Wang Lee and Dare. He tried to blackmail Dare and that's how it all started.'

Sam nodded.

'I guess he got what was coming to him. Blackmailers always end up the same way.'

Ernst snapped the brim of his hat.

'I must be running along. Murder never stops in this city — and Homicide has to keep working. Keep your nose clean, Sam.'

'Yeah, I'll do that.'

Ernst went out, leaving Sam to think of Irene. It was a couple of days later when Sam got his discharge — but he wasn't done with hospitals, yet. He caught a cab and paid a visit to Irene.

She had pulled through okay. The flesh wounds were nothing, and she had got over the shock of events. Mrs. Kline and Joey were with her when Sam walked in with a bunch of flowers. He felt embarrassed to be holding flowers instead of a gun.

'I thought you might like these,' he said.

Irene smiled.

'Of course, Sam.'

They exchanged polite, meaningless words. Sam grew more and more uncomfortable, and Irene smiled all the time. She looked very happy about something. Sam couldn't think what.

Joey polished his bald head with a handkerchief.

'I guess I'll take the air,' he said casually. He waggled his bushy eyebrows at Mrs. Kline. 'If you'd care to join me in a cup of coffee . . . ?'

Mrs. Kline was a little slow on the uptake. Joey whispered in her ear. She smiled at Sam, and murmured:

'Congratulations, Sam. I'm so glad — for both of you.'

Sam blushed for the first time in his life. He said:

'I haven't asked her yet.'

Joey took Mrs. Kline's arm as they went through the door.

Irene called: 'Thanks for everything, Joey.'

Joey said: 'It's been a pleasure,' and the door closed behind him, leaving Sam alone with Irene.

Sam said: 'Your hair's beginning to grow again. I like red hair.'

She laughed softly.

'Don't be so embarrassed, Sam — of course I love you! And you don't have to ask me anything. I've already made up my mind to marry you . . .'

Sam didn't say anything. He took her in his arms and kissed her soundly. And that was the only sound to come out of the ward for some time — the sound of two people kissing. And a gentle sigh of satisfaction. Irene Kline had found one man who wanted her.

We do hope that you have enjoyed reading this large print book.

Did you know that all of our titles are available for purchase?

We publish a wide range of high quality large print books including:
Romances, Mysteries, Classics
General Fiction
Non Fiction and Westerns

Special interest titles available in large print are:
The Little Oxford Dictionary
Music Book, Song Book
Hymn Book, Service Book

Also available from us courtesy of Oxford University Press:
Young Readers' Dictionary
(large print edition)
Young Readers' Thesaurus
(large print edition)

For further information or a free brochure, please contact us at:
Ulverscroft Large Print Books Ltd.,
The Green, Bradgate Road, Anstey,
Leicester, LE7 7FU, England.
Tel: (00 44) **0116 236 4325**
Fax: (00 44) **0116 234 0205**

Other titles in the
Linford Mystery Library:

DEATH CALLED AT NIGHT

R. A. Bennett

Jimmy Ellis believes his parents have died in a car crash when as a young boy he is taken to live with relatives in Australia. The years pass happily, then the nightmare comes. Terrifying images flit through his mind in the dark — all through the eyes of a child, a witness to grisly events seventeen years before. He begins to delve into the past, and soon he finds himself on the trail of a double murderer — a murderer who is prepared to kill again.